THE SUMMER I FELL FOR MY ENEMY

LEGACY INN

SARA JANE WOODLEY

Cover Photography By
KASPARS GRINVALDS

ELEVENTH AVENUE PUBLISHING

1
———

KIARA

"I'm home!" I call out as I shut the door, already knowing I won't get a response.

Well, that isn't entirely true. As I drop my keys in the bowl, my cat Sebastian strolls elegantly around the corner, mid-yawn and eyes half-shut. I've woken him from his late-afternoon nap.

"Hello, sir." I scratch his head. Sebastian has a dapper look, his white booties matching the little mustache under his nose. He meows loudly as I make my way to the kitchen.

"I had a great day, thank you." I pour cat food into his empty bowl. Clearly, my mom forgot to top up his food earlier today. Sebastian winds between my legs, almost tripping me, then shoves his face in the bowl and crunches away.

As soon as Sebastian is happily eating, I go to my bedroom upstairs, and drop my backpack with a loud thump. Today was the last day of school — the last day of Junior Year — and I couldn't be happier. In a year, I'll be heading into the world. In a year, I can finally leave this town. Every day is a step closer to fulfilling my dream of living literally anywhere but here.

The next chapter starts tomorrow. Every summer, Legacy Inn hires five local students. This year, I'm one of the lucky few to be selected. I'll be working as their student photographer. It's a rite of passage at Edendale High to apply for a summer job with Legacy Inn, but very few of us get these prestigious positions.

Sighing happily, I dig around the back of my closet for my suitcase and flop it open onto the bed.

"Let's see. Summer in the mountains. What does one pack?" I cock my eyebrow at Sebastian, who has devoured his food and is now rubbing against the door frame. "Any advice?"

Sebastian considers various options before perching himself on top of my pile of clean clothes.

"Smart boy." I place my camera and all of its accessories into a protective case that fits neatly in my suitcase. My trusted Fujifilm X-T4 is like a limb. It's my ticket out of this town, and it comes with me wherever I go. It's also the most expensive thing I own. I spent a year babysitting the Nightmare at the End of the Block in order to afford it. All it took was an endless amount of diapers, ear-splitting tantrums, and accepting that everything I owned would smell vaguely of spoiled milk.

I shudder at the memory, then throw jeans and sweatpants into the suitcase, along with some sweaters. I bring a bathing suit for good measure, though I don't like to swim — who knows what's swimming beneath me? And what if the algae gets tangled around my legs? The mountain lakes in Montana are known for being crystal clear and refreshing, so this is probably my best shot at swimming worry-free. But if I'm honest, I'd rather capture the lakes in photos than actually swim in them.

I want to travel and live a life of adventure, but the world terrifies me. I'm not blind to the irony; it's an internal conflict I choose to ignore.

I reluctantly throw a few dresses and skirts into the suitcase. The Inn has weddings and garden parties during the summer and, as the photographer, I must look nice to attend. Which is unfortunate — my mom discourages wearing "overly feminine" clothes. The last time I wore a dress and heels, I was so unused to the height, I sprained my ankle trying to navigate a crack in the sidewalk.

But these weddings *could* be my big break — my chance for the future of my dreams. I'm already dreading having to make conversation with all of these absurdly cheerful people going on about love. However, I know wedding photos could be the *perfect* additions to my portfolio. When put through that lens, packing dresses and makeup doesn't seem so bad.

In what feels like a matter of minutes, I'm done packing. I wander back into the kitchen, opening cupboards at random.

"Sebastian, what do you think?" I hold up a box of mac and cheese in one hand and cereal in the other. "Which would mom pick?"

Sebastian stares at me blankly, meowing loudly in response. He's sitting nicely by his bowl with his feet turned out. Always the gentleman.

His eyes dart to the mac and cheese, and it's the deciding factor. "Smart boy. You can never go wrong with cheese."

I set a pot of water on the stove, add two shakes of salt, and turn the burner to max. While I'm literally watching a pot of water and urging it to boil, I get a text from my mom.

Mom: Working late, sorry sweetie. I left a frozen lasagna from Colman's in the fridge. Directions are on the back. I should be home before you go to bed. Love you.

Too late for lasagna.

I toss my phone onto the counter, rolling my eyes. I didn't actually expect her to be here tonight, but I'm still disappointed. As the COO of Echo Home Builders, my mom is always mid-project, finishing projects, or dreaming up new projects. It would've been nice to have a last dinner together before I go away for three months.

Sebastian ambles to the center of the kitchen and dramatically flops to his side.

"Looks like you're my dinner date again." I poke his belly with my foot. He instinctively stretches out his claws and clutches my sock. After a brief skirmish, I pull away.

Glancing towards the dining table, I spot an issue of Glacier Journal lying open from yesterday. I shove it to the floor.

I'd received my rejection letter earlier today.

The Glacier Journal is a major publication in our town. Their features and editorials are circulated and shared around the world. In their last issue, they had a riveting six-page feature on a climbing expedition to Glacier National Park. The photos were unbelievable. I'm lucky to live in one of the most beautiful areas of Montana — or so people tell me — and the Glacier Journal is at the forefront of the tourism industry around here. Getting my photos published in their magazine would've been a massive step-up for me.

Awards, photo prints, and framed originals adorn the walls of our house — all work I've done over the years. This past year, I even had a couple photos featured in our town's gazette. I win awards for photography with our school's newspaper every year. Actually, this year's award sits heavily at the bottom of my backpack. The photo was a particularly engaging shot that went viral in my high school — or as viral as can be in Edendale. And, as with anything that goes viral, it caused a few problems, which I choose to ignore.

I applied for Glacier thinking that I'd be a shoo-in. I sent them my best and brightest photos taken around the area. Once, I set up my camera as a storm rolled in and captured photos as the storm hit. Unfortunately, the rain came *much* sooner than expected, and I squelched home as wet as if I'd showered fully clothed. The other photo I sent was of a herd of elk. I sat in my car for 10 straight hours, waiting for the shot, sustained by Pepsi and Nacho Cheese Doritos.

Glacier Journal was the first major magazine I'd applied to. And it fell flat, to my utter disappointment.

I finish making my mac and cheese, then take a seat at the table. My dinner date, Sebastian, remains on the floor, snoring gently. I dig into my bowl of steaming mac and cheese and flip open the Legacy Inn's marketing brochure, perusing the photos. They aren't *bad* photos by any stretch of the imagination, they just seem outdated.

I chuckle at a photo of a big fish and remember my conversation with Ava earlier today.

"You? Going out in nature?" Ava laughed and closed her locker for the last time this year. She lugged her violin in one hand and the rest of her gear in her other hand.

"Is that so hard to believe? Wait. Don't answer that." I grabbed Ava's violin while she juggled the rest of her stuff. Ava is my best friend at Edendale High School. We have a similar love for art — me for photography, her for music.

"Legacy Inn is my chance to strengthen my portfolio," I said as we walked the halls. "It's surrounded by lakes, forests, mountains, all that outdoor stuff. I'll be able to take some killer nature shots!"

Ava laughed again, her curly hair bouncing with every step. "Says the girl who only visits the mountains on an annual basis."

"What's the rush? It's not like they're going anywhere." I smirk, but I know she's right. "I'll visit the mountains everyday if it means becoming a photographer and getting the chance to travel the world. Plus, there'll be weddings and events. Av, think of the floofy white dresses."

Ava snorts. "The girl who loves the indoors and despises formal wear is heading out for a summer of mountains and marriages."

"Mountains, marriages, and *photography*. Don't forget the most important part."

Photos are my everything.

I scrape the bottom of the bowl to catch the last piece of lingering macaroni. I'll miss Ava when I go to Legacy Inn, but I know she'll be busy with band camp this summer. All she has are her big dreams and violin, but when you have determination like hers, that's all you need.

I flip through the Inn's brochure again, my anticipation building. The Legacy Inn and it's surrounding area are stunning, even if the photos in the brochure are outdated. I can only imagine the amazing lifestyle and nature shots I'll be taking this summer with my pro camera. Glacier will be knocking down my door for photos.

Tomorrow is the first day of the rest of my life.

I'm counting down the minutes.

2

JONATHAN

"*T*his is your chance to shine, Jonathan," Dad's voice reverberates around our dining room table.

I have one piece of pasta left on my plate and I shift it around in circles, gazing at it as though watching the best soccer match of the season. Usually, these dinners go by quickly if I keep my head down and nod frequently. I tune in and out of the conversation, knowing that the topic is about me but doesn't necessarily include me.

"Alan, he knows that." Mom flips her blonde bobbed hair over her shoulder. She's still wearing her work clothes. The meal feels more like a college interview than a family dinner. And I would know, with all the training they've been putting me through. "He'll work hard at soccer camp this summer. Won't you, Jonathan?"

"Definitely," I say robotically. I toss the final piece of pasta into my mouth. The cheesy pasta dish we had for dinner was a "reward" for all of my hard work on my school's soccer team.

Mom whipped up the meal while she was ranting about how summer training camps groom high schoolers for college soccer. When I got home, I didn't have time to drop my backpack in my room, or tell her about my last day of school. My parents are determined to make sure I'm ready for training camp tomorrow. Apparently, this means emphasizing how much this will *change everything and set the course of my life in a new and exciting direction.* They've memorized the marketing material verbatim.

"All I'm saying is that, if you do well, we could be looking at a phenomenal scholarship. You had a great junior year — state champion MVP. But this is the next step. Show them what you can do as a midfielder and you'll get a full-ride at the best colleges in the country."

With the amount of times I've heard my dad say this over the past month, I'm starting to think I'm living the movie Groundhog Day.

Meanwhile, he has pasta stuck in his mustache and I'm keeping tabs to see when it falls off.

My acceptance letter for Momentum Soccer Camp came in the mail a month ago, and my parents have hardly spoken of anything else since. The past few weeks have been all about Momentum and how this is my big break. There was one day that we *didn't* speak about Momentum, but it was only because my parents were fawning over our win in the State Finals. The Edendale Eagles brought home the gold once again.

The funny thing? I never applied for Momentum — my parents applied for me. If I had my pick, I would have done any number of things this summer that did not involve soccer. My love for soccer died around the time my junior coach mentioned I had a future in the sport and my parents started forcing me into regular 6am workouts.

Given their excitement, I didn't want to let them down

by opting not to go to Momentum. So I said I'd go. And I meant it.

At least, I did until three days ago.

A break comes in their conversation about the glory of Momentum, and I take advantage of the silence. I jump up from the table, clear my plate and put it in the dishwasher, then grab my backpack off the counter.

"Going to my room." I swipe a chocolate bar from my mom's hidden stash. I'm supposed to regulate sugar intake, and my mom is monitoring my diet for optimal performance, but there's only so much grilled chicken and broccoli a guy can take.

The chocolate bar is out of the wrapper and in my mouth before I even make it to my bedroom. I close my eyes and savor the rich taste, grateful that I can have as many cheat days as I want this summer.

My room is sparkling clean and my suitcase is open on my bed, soccer cleats carefully positioned on top. Looks like Mom got a head start.

With a sigh, I open my phone and see a message from Troy, my best friend.

Troy: Yo, have you told your parents?

Jonathan: No way. Dad's head would explode and Mom would launch into her classic "after everything we've done for you" guilt trip. No thanks. As far as you know, I'm at Momentum this summer.

Troy: K, have a good time bro, keep in touch.

I stash my phone and haphazardly stuff clothes into my suitcase. I fold my soccer jersey, cleats and other gear nicely on top, in case my mom opens my suitcase later. I know my parents mean well, but the next three months can't come fast enough.

Troy is the only one who knows where I'm going this

summer. He's the best defender on the Edendale Eagles, and he's planning on applying for Momentum next year. This summer, he's sticking around town and doing recon for me, making sure no one finds out my secret.

As my parents said, I am leaving tomorrow.

But what they don't know is that I won't be going to Momentum Soccer Camp.

3

KIARA

*T*he rumble of the bus lulls me into a daydream. I left the house early this morning to catch the first bus out of town. Now, looking out the window, music blaring through my headphones, the landscape changes before my eyes. The city of Edendale gives way to the foothills, and the foothills to mountains. Periodically, I lift my camera to my face and snap a photo of the scenery.

An hour later, I'm standing in a rustic cabin at the secluded Legacy Inn.

If you can call it a cabin. It's a small A-frame structure with a bed, a dresser, a desk and two big windows with blackout curtains. It's so cozy, I took photos of the cabin before moving in. Nothing like minimalistic Montana decor.

It takes me all of 15 minutes to unpack my bags and make myself at home. I change into my jean shorts and an old T-shirt before layering on the bug spray and sunscreen.

I step onto my tiny balcony and assess the small community I've joined. Six cabins are set up in a semicircle near the edge of the grounds. Five students are coming this summer, so the sixth cabin is likely an office or storage space. Three of the cabins have their doors open, meaning that three students from Edendale have already moved in.

"Please don't let them be chatty," I mutter to myself.

There are about 500 students in my grade at Edendale High School. While I know everyone by their faces, I make a point not to know them on a personal level. Putting down roots in Edendale has never been a part of the plan. In recent years, I have made only one exception — Ava. And she's the only exception I intend to make.

I skip down the steps leading to my cabin and stroll along the gravel path that leads to the main building. Despite the threat of bugs, it's a lovely spot. Flowers line the path and little copses of trees create a sense of seclusion. The trickling of a creek in the background adds to the serene ambiance.

A pink wildflower stands through the gravel, the color vibrant compared to the surrounding grey. I kneel to take a photo.

The Inn looms in front of me. It's a magnificent 2-level structure made entirely of rich redwood and built to resemble a gigantic log cabin. Two wings with guest rooms shoot off from either side of the main building. The main building itself has big, sleek windows and a large open-air balcony. On the lower level, the porch opens onto a beautiful garden with an outdoor bar.

The garden weddings must be wonderful. I walk tentatively through the garden and note the beautiful flowers in pots all around. A lady tending to the flowers waves at me, a friendly smile on her face, and I hesitantly wave back.

The whole place buzzes with energy, fueling my mission to find Delia, the Inn's manager. She told me to come and find her after unpacking my stuff. I walk over the porch and into the Inn, bypassing the man and woman playfully bickering about a broken panel on the deck.

Inside the Inn, I wander through the games room before finding my way upstairs to the event room. Finally, I spot a slim woman with work jeans, a colorful top, and hair pulled into a tight white bun. She's speaking to one of the chefs.

"A cheeseburger taco? I LOVE IT! Feature them in the July menu, please and thank you, Fernando." Delia gestures wildly as she speaks. The chef — Fernando? — ducks under one of her waving hands and disappears towards the kitchen.

"Delia?" My voice is timid. I clear my throat and stand straight, remembering what my mom taught me about appearing confident even when you don't feel it. I try again. "All unpacked!"

Delia whips around, her hands flying through the air.

I duck. It's a good thing — if I hadn't, Delia would've accidentally slapped me.

"Ah, yes! Kira."

"It's Ki-ara, actually."

"That's the one. Come!" Delia abruptly turns, making a beeline for the balcony. "We are in dire need of a strong pair of hands."

I jog after Delia as she strides across the event room floor. She can't be younger than 50, but I'm practically out of breath trying to keep up. She maneuvers through the tables with the grace of a swan while I stumble along with the grace of a four-year-old trying to wear their mom's high heels.

Delia stops abruptly by the far wall, which is made almost entirely of windows.

"Is that a spot?" She peers at one of the panes and rubs

her thumb over the glass. I'm not sure if she's speaking to me. She leans in closer and I almost lean in with her before she pops back up again. "I'll get Vin on that right away."

Delia opens the door onto the massive balcony and strides outside with me in tow. "So, Kira-"

"Ki-ara."

"Do you see that gazebo down there?" She points to a gathering of trees in the distance.

"Not quite?" I squint to see through the trees.

"Ah, it's down there." She swats her hand in the general direction of the gazebo. "We need to hang some fairy lights in the gazebo in preparation for tonight's Welcome Bash."

Her green eyes sparkle over her half-moon glasses and a smile comes over my face. This lady is chaotic, but in the best way.

"Right, the Welcome Bash." I'm not looking forward to the event, but I know it will be an opportunity to take photos of everyone milling about and celebrating.

"It's all hands on deck here, my dear!" Delia casts a glance over the grounds of the Inn. "The fairy lights are just down by the gazebo. All you have to do is hang them up. Okay? Okay. If you have any questions, just pull me or Vin aside. Now Vin... where did he go?"

As dramatically as Delia first appeared, she strides off, back into the event room.

Blindsided by the Inn manager's energy, I take a moment to gaze out over the grounds. The gathering of trees — where the gazebo *should* be — is right next to the lake.

Guests must spend their days canoeing or rafting on the lake before coming back to shore and relaxing on the private beach. A pathway snakes along the lakeshore, continuing around the periphery of Legacy Lake. In the distance, white mountain peaks jut elegantly towards the sky.

It must be such a cool place to spend a summer. A bolt of excitement flies through me as I realize that this very spot might hold the key to my future.

4

KIARA

*a*fter almost getting lost trying to exit the Inn, I finally emerge onto the porch. I stroll through the garden, smiling at the lady with the flowerpots, and head towards the lake.

By the shore, I spot a girl I recognize from school — I think her name is Anaya. She's standing next to the dock, looking lost. I give her a little wave and she waves back.

The trees by the lake all look the same to me. After looking back and forth for some clarity, I catch sight of a sign and thank my lucky stars. Goodness knows I have *no* sense of direction.

I follow the signs all the way to the dainty white gazebo by the lake. The gravel path continues past the gazebo and I realize that this is the path I took to enter the grounds. It will take a lot of work not to get lost here. My head is already spinning.

A cardboard box sits next to the gazebo, with tangled fairy lights inside. There are hooks around the ceiling, and I decide to take some creative liberties with hanging the lights.

I stand on my tiptoes to hang a strand of lights, but I'm too short. I'm comfortable with my height of 5'7", but it won't do me any good today.

There's a step ladder off to the side, and, with its help, I hang the first string of lights. I make my way around the gazebo, carefully stringing the lights and humming. The final string of lights will require some acrobatics — I want to braid it through the others to create a doily shape.

I carefully place my camera on the railing. I'm absolutely not going to risk dropping it.

I climb to the highest level of the stepladder. It wobbles slightly.

"Careful, Kiara, careful," I say. I stand on my tiptoes. The lights are almost braided through—

And that's when I lose my balance.

I yelp as my foot rolls, and I slip off the stepladder.

I tumble towards the balcony railing, holding my hands out instinctively as I fall.

I brace for impact, squeezing my eyes shut.

Suddenly, an arm circles my midsection. Shocked, I open my eyes in time to see my hand hit my camera, knocking it off the railing and sending it hurtling towards the ground.

No!

I shriek.

I scramble towards the railing, falling out the grasp of the person holding me up.

My camera stops in midair.

The person, my mysterious rescuer, has grasped the camera strap. My beloved camera is dangling in the air, whole and unbroken.

I let out a cry of relief. "Thank you!"

This person saved my butt. Breaking my camera would

have meant losing this job and derailing my plans for the future. I whip around, leaning in to give the person a hug—

Then I realize who saved me.

KIARA

*M*y rescuer is Jonathan Wright.

No. No. Anyone — ANYONE — but him. My face crinkles in anguish. Of all the people to save me, to save my camera, why did it have to be Jonathan fricking Wright?

And why is he even here? Shouldn't he be prancing around a soccer field and bragging about how good he is at kicking a stupid ball into a useless net?

"Oh," I say unenthusiastically, meeting his denim blue eyes. "Thanks."

His sandy blonde hair has that casual bedhead look that I bet he spent hours trying to perfect. He's holding me tight against his body, steadying me after the fall. Within seconds, his gaze goes from shock to mild irritation.

I step out of his grasp at the same time that he drops his arm. Without a word, he hands me my camera. I wrap the strap tight around my midsection.

Jonathan and I have been in school together for years, and our dislike for one another has grown steadily over time. In fact, I can't remember a time that I *liked* Jonathan.

Maybe we were friends back in the days of toys and sand-boxes. But now? He's your typical star athlete, getting every-thing he could ever want in life.

"You know guests aren't allowed here until tomorrow," I say curtly, my hand on my hips. Ugh. Why did *he* have to play hero? It would've been better to fall.

"Good thing I'm not a guest." He brushes a piece of lint off his designer label shirt, an innocent gesture that somehow makes me loathe him even more.

He slings his duffel bag over his shoulder like it weighs nothing. "You might want to be careful with your camera. Those things are expensive."

Before I can say anything, he turns and skips out of the gazebo.

My blood boils as he walks away. Who is *he* to tell *me* to be careful around expensive things? I may not know Jonathan well, but I don't think anyone else does either. Very few people have seen the side of him that I've seen...

The Inn should be staffed up for the summer. So why is he here?

And what did he mean that he's not a guest?

There's no way he's working here... right?

JONATHAN

I stride down the gravel path towards the Inn, reeling from my encounter with Kiara the Queen.

When I approached her in the gazebo, I had no idea it was her. Sure, now I recognize the wavy brown hair, the tanned skin, the slim figure. But I've never seen Kiara in shorts before, and never without her beloved camera slung around her neck.

I got there just in time. I saw her roll her ankle and knew she was about to topple. I grabbed her waist and then went for the camera. Good reflexes are one perk of being an athlete, I guess. Though now, knowing it was her, I'm not sure I would've tried so hard to save the camera.

Kiara and I have known each other for a long time and I have good reason to dislike her. She has this infuriating way of acting like she's better than everyone else, hence the nickname "Kiara the Queen". The Eagles' top striker, Lucas, coined it for her last fall.

At Edendale High, she's alienated almost everyone except for her one friend, Ava. They usually hang out in the artsy side of school, where the photo room is located. In class, I've noticed that she's one of those "intelligent slacker" students. You know the type — they sleep through class and then get an A on the final exam while stifling yawns.

The problem is, Kiara's so blunt and straightforward that it's intimidating. I heard she's even made teachers cry.

I shake myself off as I walk through a garden leading to the Inn. I didn't do a good job of vetting which students would be here this summer. I never would've expected the Queen to climb down from her throne and roll up her sleeves.

Ahead, a lady struggles with a flowerpot. I drop my bag and jog over.

"Here, let me." I help her lift the flowerpot onto a table.

"Aren't you sweet?" she says, removing one of her gloves to shake my hand. "I'm Nath, it's lovely to meet ya."

Nath looks to be about my mom's age, but her skin is tanned and she has smile lines around her mouth. My mom got rid of her smile lines a few years ago. Somehow, I found her more beautiful then, but I would never say so.

"Pleasure's mine. I'm Jonathan." I smile. "Do you know where I can find Delia?"

Nath points up to the balcony of the Inn. "Last I saw her she was buzzing around upstairs, but you never quite know where that one's going to end up."

Thanking Nath, I walk into the Inn, stepping into what appears to be a games room.

I'm momentarily distracted by the pool table. It's been a while since I played pool — my parents never wanted me to play in case of "injuries", but I break that rule whenever the opportunity comes up. Lucas has a pool table at his house, and whenever he hosts parties, I always make an appearance. I'm not a big partier, but I do love to play a game or two.

"Hello there!" A loud voice calls to me from across the room. A friendly-looking lady with white hair and blue jeans strides purposefully towards me. "You must be Johnny. John?"

"Jonathan." I beam back at her, recognizing her voice instantly. "Delia?"

"In the flesh." Behind her, a slight man with black hair and warm eyes steps forward. "And this is Vin."

I nod a greeting towards Vin as Delia continues. "It was quite the surprise getting your call just a couple of days ago. We had only *just* talked about hiring another student when — ding — there you were! You know what I think it was? Fate. And I'll admit that was part of the reason we hired you. When the universe sends you a message, you gotta listen."

She winks theatrically. Behind her back, Vin rolls his eyes. Delia senses his reaction and turns to swat him playfully.

I hold back a laugh.

"It's great to have you here, Jonathan. We've set up another cabin for you just outside. We put it together pretty quickly so if something's missing or something doesn't quite work, let us know and we can get right on fixing that."

Delia clutches her clipboard to her chest. "We have lots to do before the Welcome Bash tonight so why don't you get set up and then come back here to help the chefs in the kitchen? Vin'll show you the way to your cabin."

With that, Delia sets off towards the staircase.

"She's really got everything under control, hey?" I say to Vin as we head out the door.

Vin laughs. "She's a ball of chaos. She *seems* to be all

over the map, but somehow, everything falls into place. You just have to trust the Delia way."

When we get to the summer student area on the far side of the grounds, Vin shows me into a cabin on the edge of a semicircle of similar structures. It's a sparse space, and a part of me misses the computer, phone and tablet I have at home.

I place my bag in the cabin and step out onto the small balcony. A couple of fellow students are milling about, but no one I know well. In the center of the semicircle of cabins, there's a cement platform with a picnic table and chairs. A couple of hammocks sway in the trees nearby. The chill atmosphere feels unfamiliar but comfortable.

I have a feeling I'll enjoy my time here at the Inn — as long as I tiptoe around Kiara the Queen.

KIARA

*M*y blood is still boiling as I make my way out of the Inn later that afternoon. I can't stop thinking about *him*. What on earth is Jonathan Wright doing here? *Why* is he working here? Shouldn't the golden boy be off playing soccer or whatever?

"I just wanted a couple of months *away* from all of that." I look to the sky, frustrated.

While the opportunity to take awesome photos drew me to Legacy Inn, I also came to escape the drudgery of life in Edendale, where the high school cliques and clichés run wild. And now, to have to spend the entire summer with the very person who sits at the core of the entitled elite! *Ugh.*

I resolve to stay as far away from him as possible over the next few months. Jonathan's likely just doing maintenance work or something, if he *is* working here. He shouldn't be hard to avoid.

Besides, I have more important things to think about — my dreams, my future, my career. This summer, I need to focus on improving my photography. Legacy Inn is teeming with chances to take beautiful nature and lifestyle images.

Jonathan is a today problem, but in a year, when I'm far away from here, he'll be a speck in the rearview mirror as I barrel towards my exciting life.

I stroll to the lakeshore and follow the gravel path circling the water. After stringing up the last of the fairy lights in the gazebo, I helped with a few more tasks around the Inn, including dusting the pool table in the games room and helping decorate the event room.

Now, everyone's inside, getting ready for the Welcome Bash. But I want to take advantage of the peace and quiet around the lake.

I aim the camera, adjust focus, and capture the scenery. I take photos of a group of ducks swimming out from the shore with their ducklings, the lime green of the leaves as the sun shines through them, the clear reflection of the mountain peaks in the lake. It's easy to see why people visit the Inn in the summer.

The path turns a corner, and the Inn drops out of sight as a small mountain rises next to me. There must be some fantastic viewpoints for photos up there.

On a mission, I continue along the gravel path, looking for a side path that would lead up the mountain. Unfortunately, I can't see anything but dense brush and lush forest. *Way* too much nature.

I step back and observe the mountain once again.

Ah, who am I kidding? Even if there was a path, I wouldn't climb the mountain. I'm not a big hiker, and heights? No thanks. I won't even jump off a diving board.

I eye the mountain and try to ignore the pang of sadness needling me. I used to hike with my parents when I was a kid. My parents were very adventurous, but when my dad left, everything changed. Mom buried herself in work, and I buried myself in photography.

You've got to find your best way to cope. For me, that meant taking care of myself and learning to be independent. Learning to enjoy my life, have fun and be carefree? That can come when I fulfill my dreams.

Like my mom always says: there's no time for love if you're not *doing* what you love. In my case, love comes in the form of my future as a photographer.

"Someday, I will climb you," I say to the mountain, not knowing what point in the future I'm referencing. Could be tomorrow, could be 20 years from now.

"Well, isn't that romantic?" A deep voice says from beside me and I almost jump out of my skin.

I whirl around to find myself face to face with Jonathan. He smirks like he's just caught me doing something deeply embarrassing. I suppose he has. It's not every day that you come across someone speaking to a mountain.

"So, are you just following me around now?" I ask. My face burns red, but I'm hoping the shadows conceal it.

"Someone needs to keep an eye on you. Just in case you need rescuing again." Jonathan shrugs with practiced nonchalance. He's wearing the same fancy polo shirt and slacks he wears at school. "You realize it's a free country and you don't *own* this lake?"

I exhale in a huff and put my camera back up to my face, pretending to line up the lake for a photo. "I don't *own* this lake. But I was hand-selected to take photos of it all summer. And what will *you* be doing, golden boy? Maintenance or something?"

"Yeah... something."

I almost open my mouth to ask him what he means, but that's exactly what he wants me to do. Instead, I keep my mouth shut and flip my hair over my shoulder as I turn away. The girls in movies make it look so cool, but with my wild wavy hair, I probably look like a shampoo commercial reject.

I sashay down the path towards our cabins. Or what I hope is the path to our cabins. I'm holding my head high, which unfortunately means I don't see the rock sticking up on the path. I stub my toe and stumble, but I try to skip out of it so it looked to be purposeful.

"Careful," Jonathan calls, his voice dripping with sarcasm. "I won't always be around to save you."

My face burns.

There will be no peace as long as Jonathan's here.

JONATHAN

*K*iara marches down the path towards the Inn, swinging her hips back and forth. The display reminds me of my ex-girlfriend, Isabella, trying to walk sexy.

I hold back a chuckle, knowing that this was probably not her intent. She stumbles over a rock and makes a quick save, walking with even more purpose. I roll my eyes and take a jab at her. We might not be in high school, but she still acts like royalty.

I gaze out over the huge, oval lake. The mountains frame its outline, and their reflection mirrors in the glassy blue water. It's picture perfect — I can see why Kiara was out here taking photos. It's a beautiful evening, calm and serene. I haven't heard this loud sort of quiet in a very long time, and I haven't been able to stop and enjoy it since I was a kid.

After unpacking my bag, a walk was the perfect way to unwind. The bare cabin with just a dresser and bed felt oddly comfortable after I'd moved in. Back home, my dad's fancy car and my mom's expensive jewelry come first. But this new minimalist lifestyle agrees with me.

I stashed my soccer gear deep in the bottom of my dresser. I won't be looking at those or using them all summer. As I closed the drawer, my shoulders fell, and for the first time in forever, I felt myself relax.

I'm no stranger to lightly rebelling against my parents' wishes, but I've never blatantly disregarded their plans for me. I have never straight up lied to them. But this might be my only chance to take control of my future. I told them I'll be busy at Momentum and I won't be able to contact them often. That should keep them off my trail. They wouldn't *dare* risk hurting my chances at getting a scholarship.

I pick up a rock by the lakeshore and skip it into the water, disturbing the perfect reflection. Before the surface can still, I turn and walk back along the path to our cabins, my sense of unease steadily growing.

There's a familiar object near the picnic table — a lone soccer ball, tucked beneath a bush, abandoned by an earlier set of players. I toe the ball out and mindlessly dribble, skillfully touching the top of the ball with my left foot, before turning and dragging the ball forward with my other foot, quickly turning again to finish. I had practiced this piece of footwork — the Maradona — thousands of times, until my execution was flawless.

Sure, Momentum felt like a dream come true, but I recently realized that the dream was not my own. So instead, I came here. And I can say, with confidence, that I've never felt so out of my depths. I'm nervous about what this summer will bring.

In soccer, the moves come like breathing. There's no thinking, no doubting. It's an instinct that lives within me, that's part of me. At school, if I put my head down, I get good grades. I'm not the best in my classes, by far, but I do well. If I didn't have soccer to carry me through to college, my grades would still get me somewhere. Sometimes, I wish I could apply to college without mentioning my soccer skills, without being the MVP of the state champion soccer team. But I also know how important this full-ride scholarship is for my parents.

I dribble the ball around the green patch of grass next to the picnic table. This summer is my chance to do something different. This is my opportunity to challenge myself, to feel something more than passive happiness when our team wins a game. For the first time in a long time, the stakes are high and I'm wondering: Can I do this?

I kick the ball a little too hard. It flies underneath the cabin next to mine, getting lost in the darkness. I sigh. I'll have to grab it later. I duck into my cabin to get ready.

I throw on my slacks and a polo shirt before realizing that no one here will care what I wear to the Welcome Bash. I hesitantly put on board shorts instead, feeling happy with the change.

It's now or never, Jonathan. I grab one last item from my duffel bag and make my way to the event room.

JONATHAN

*T*he Welcome Bash is a burst of catchy songs, colorful flowers, and beautiful string lights. Walking inside the Inn feels like walking into a folk music video. Whoever did the decorations did a brilliant job.

Staffers mingle and get to know the student workers. I recognize a few kids from school, but no one I know well. That's by design — before asking for the job here, I made sure that none of my close friends or teammates would be working at the Inn over the summer. As far as they know, I'm at Momentum, just like I told my parents. Troy is the only one who knows where I am, but I haven't told him *why* I'm here.

The scent of roasted garlic and freshly-baked cheese bread makes my stomach grumble. I may not be playing soccer this summer, but I still have the appetite of a bear. And working with the chefs today kick-started the hunger.

I make a beeline for the food table. But, before I can get my paws on a slice of cheese bread, Delia bursts through the crowd, her colorful dress flowing and her cowboy hat tilted on her head.

"Jonathan! Thank you for your help in the kitchen. The food smells wonderful." Delia kisses her fingertips as though she's straight out of Italy. "Fernando was raving about how you lifted two gigantic bags of flour with one arm. We might have you help out around the kitchen, my boy!"

"Happy to." I smile. Poor Fernando almost threw his back out lifting the first bag of flour.

"That's the attitude I want to see!" Delia tips her cowboy hat and swoops away.

With Delia gone, I return to my mission: Food.

Nath stands near the foot of the table, plate in hand. She's talking to a girl from Edendale High — Stefanie?

"Jonathan? And he's not on the field or wearing cleats? Something must be wrong." Stefanie looks at me skeptically and pretends to rub her eyes as if she can't believe what she's seeing.

Nath laughs. "Nice to see you, Jon — can I call you Jon?"

"Oh, Jonathan's fine." I say with a smile. Only my teammates call me Jon.

Nath nods, smiling. "Jonathan it is. Stefi was telling me that you were the MVP for the state championship? That's very exciting! Go Eagles!"

"Thanks, totally a team effort," I say, laughing sheepishly. I wish that star label wouldn't follow me around. "How're you doing, Stefi?"

Stefi runs with the high-achieving crowd at Edendale High. I don't know the group well, aside from when we share the occasional group project.

"Good, excited to work here this summer," Stefi says, looking around the room. "We're lucky to have these positions!"

"Definitely."

Nath takes a slice of cheese bread. "What kind of work will you be doing at the Inn, Jonathan?"

Stefi and Nath look at me expectantly and I freeze. I'm racking my brain trying to voice my answer when I'm saved by Vin. He's motioning from across the room for me to meet the guy he's speaking with.

"Oh, ya know, just helping out," I say as I step away. "Anyway, guys, it looks like I'm being summoned. I'll catch up with you later."

I'm filled with relief as I make my way towards Vin. It's not that my job here is a secret, but I don't feel ready to see their faces and deal with the confusion. The older staff here at the Inn won't be a problem, but the kids from school? They'll have questions. And I'm not ready to answer those yet.

In the corner of my eye, I see Kiara enter the event room, bringing a late spring frost with her. She wears shorts and a hoodie, her hair tied into a strict ponytail. It trips me up to see her in shorts. It implies that she enjoys something other than photography — maybe she actually likes summer.

If only I'd properly checked the list of students coming to the Inn. There wasn't much holding me back from coming here, but Kiara the Queen? I would've stayed away from her palace to avoid the chopping block.

KIARA

*T*he Welcome Bash is well underway by the time I set off from my cabin. I'm not exactly punctual at the best of times. But for a party? My arrival time hedges between fashionably late and not bothering to show up at all.

Ava and I attend the odd party at Edendale High, but it's a very different scene. Those gatherings consist of a small group of art students discussing life, politics, philosophy and other high-minded topics. The more musically inclined take up their guitars, harps, flutes or other instruments to provide a soundtrack for the evening. The gatherings are chill. A guy like Jonathan Wright would never come to one of our parties.

I've heard the big blowouts put on by the Eagles get crazy. Jonathan and his group of friends seem bent on destroying their livers and wasting their weekends, regardless of the consequences.

The Welcome Bash won't be anything like those big blowouts, but it won't resemble the small art gatherings I've attended, either.

The event room is exactly as I envisioned it. Fairy lights rise and fall between wooden beams on the ceiling, casting the room in a delicate glow. Lanterns and paper flowers hang from hooks and make everything feel like summer. A fresh mountain breeze flows through the space, courtesy of the propped open balcony doors.

I'm enjoying the scene right up until Jonathan crosses my path. He glares at me, so I glare right back. I will not let him distract me from my goals this summer.

On that, I lift my camera and start taking photos of the event as it unfolds.

"You must be Kiara," a warm voice says. I turn to look into the brown eyes of the lady from the garden. "I'm Nath, it's a pleasure to meet ya."

"Me too," I say brightly, and then immediately regret my choice of words. I give her a sheepish smile and unclasp my hand from my camera, extending it to her. She laughs and shakes it. *Nice one, Kiara.*

She eyes my camera. "So, you're doing photography this summer?"

I reluctantly release the camera and let it hang from the neck strap, awkwardly placing my hands on my hips. I smile. "That's right."

Nath and I stand in silence. I'm not sure what to say next, or if anything needs to be said at all. Small talk is a skill I have no desire to master. My eyes linger on Jonathan and I glare as he speaks with people at the far end of the room. They laugh at something he says.

Must be nice to be able to charm your way through everything.

"You go to Edendale High, Kiara?" Nath asks, drawing me from my thoughts.

"Unfortunately, yes," I say, smiling slyly. "I'm excited to graduate."

Nath laughs, "I know a couple of Edendale kids pretty well. I just met a lovely girl — Stefi. And there's the boy over there, Jonathan. Are you friends with either of them?"

My smile falters. The golden boy strikes again, charming everyone with his act. I'll give him this — he's very good at putting on a front. I suppose it must be easier to act charming when you have everything you want given to you on a silver platter.

"Stefi seems sweet," I respond, my eyes back on Jonathan. He's chatting to a couple of guys with a big smile on his face and not a care in the world. How I'd love to paste a "kick me" sign to his back. "But Jonathan and I are definitely *not* friends."

Nath chuckles and her voice drops low, her next words an afterthought. "I remember when my husband and I were definitely *not* friends. Which reminds me, you should come and meet Vin."

She drags me across the room, and if it isn't just my luck, Vin is one of the people Jonathan is speaking with. I don't recognize the other guy, but he looks about my age.

"Vin, this is Kiara. She's the last of the Edendale summer students." Nath positions me in front of Vin. He's a slight man with kind eyes and a big smile.

"Welcome to Legacy Inn, very happy to have you here." Vin shakes my hand. "I was getting caught up with Jonathan and Wes here. Wes'll be going to Edendale High in the fall."

Wes's tanned face crinkles into a smile. He has clear turquoise eyes and blonde, sun-bleached hair.

"Surprise, surprise, you still have your camera." Jonathan's voice drips with sarcasm.

"Almost as surprising as seeing your face without Isabella attached to it," I reply.

"We all make mistakes," Jonathan says. "But, now that my face is unoccupied, figure I'll go stuff it with some of that cheese bread. You in, Wes?"

They say their goodbyes and stride across the room. Vin and Nath seem nice, so I spend a few minutes chatting with them. They're long-time staffers at the Inn and they actually met here years ago.

"Can I take some photos of you guys?" I ask on a whim. They've both got a dreamy, romantic look on their faces as they rehash how they met.

"Only if you get my good side," Vin says.

Nath pats his arm. "Oh, honey, that photography trick only works if you have a good side."

Vin frowns. "But dear, I thought that *you* were my good side?"

Nath rolls her eyes and sighs. "Ever the charmer."

They look into each other's eyes and giggle like they're school kids with a secret crush. It's the perfect moment to capture.

We part ways and I circulate, taking more photos as the crowd unwinds. It's a beautiful setting and I'm incredibly inspired. I can't wait to take photos of the events and other special occasions happening here over the summer. Double feature in Glacier Journal, here I come!

As I move about the periphery of the room, I avoid Jonathan. He's in the heart of it all, meeting and chatting with everyone. He has this undeniable charisma — this charm — that captivates everyone around him. I can only imagine how easy life must be for a guy like him.

I consider my own past, such a contrast to Jonathan's. When my father left, we fell on hard times and we had to buckle down and save every penny we got. My mom finally got a job with Echo as a project manager and she quickly worked her way to the top.

It's pure luck that working in construction has always been her dream. But it sure wasn't an easy path to get there.

Delia claps her hands, bringing everyone's attention to the front of the event room. She stands on the lip of the fireplace, a friendly smile on her face. Her colorful flowing dress, black vest, and black cowboy hat accentuate her long, white hair.

"Good evening, everyone!" Her voice carries easily through the room. "And welcome to another summer at the Legacy Inn!"

Small whoops erupt from the crowd.

Delia tips her cowboy hat. "We're delighted to have you here this summer. Vin and I have been hard at work planning this Welcome Bash, and we couldn't have executed it without all of your help! So thank you, one and all, for making this event such a success."

More applause. I drop my camera for a second to clap along.

"The guests arrive tomorrow. There's nothing like summer at the Legacy Inn. This is going to be a busy, hectic, wonderful three months. I can't wait to experience it with all of you."

Delia explains some ground rules for the summer, but I tune them out. Jonathan is standing just ahead of me and I can now see that he's holding a little black bag with a white label. The bag looks familiar and my stomach churns uneasily.

Is that what I think it is?

"And now, we'll introduce our student workers for the summer. Many of you have already met, but in case you haven't, here they are!" Delia says.

She starts announcing the list of students from Edendale High School, but it's hard for me to focus when my curiosity is pulling me towards golden boy's little black bag. I slowly approach, trying to glimpse the label on the side.

"Kiara Garcia!" Delia calls my name and I snap to attention. Darn, just missed my chance.

I make my way to the front of the room and stand next to the other students. I count five of us, so I wonder where Jonathan fits in.

"At the last minute, we decided to hire a sixth student this summer — Jonathan Wright!" Delia answers my question and Jonathan walks through the crowd.

My heart sinks to my toes. Jonathan Wright *will* be working here. It's like having your best dream invaded by your worst nightmare. How could this get any worse?

Jonathan comes to stand in the spot next to me and I refrain from stepping away from him.

"The Inn has been doing extremely well in recent years," Delia says. "It's a testament to all of your hard work. We thought it was time to hire another student to help out." The older staff members, the ones who are here full-time, cheer and applaud.

Delia goes on, a big smile on her face. "Given how successful the Inn has been, we've decided..." Delia pauses for effect, gesturing towards Vin. "We want to take entirely new photos of the Inn and revamp our marketing and branding. We'll also be posting new photos on our social media accounts daily!"

I'm sorry, what? I had no idea Legacy Inn was considering a rebrand. I can barely contain my excitement.

New photos of the Inn? Redoing all of their brochures with new images? Posting photos to their social media? This is the kind of exposure that can launch me into my future.

My heart races. This project is exactly what I'm looking for.

As my mind fills with images and possibilities of what I can do to capture the spirit of the Inn, I barely hear Delia's next few words.

"For this reason, we thought it would be fun to hire two student photographers this year."

My jaw drops and my hopes come violently crashing down around me.

No.

No no no.

Delia pauses again, the room silent.

My thoughts are an angry storm.

Delia gestures towards me. No, not towards me. Towards me and *him*. "Jonathan and Kiara will be working together this summer to redo all of our imagery!"

This can't be happening.

Jonathan opens the little black bag and takes out his very own camera. The same camera that I worked so, so hard to afford.

My face turns white as a sheet and my legs go numb.

Do I seriously have to spend my summer working with Jonathan fricking Wright?!

11

JONATHAN

*M*y camera strap sits heavy around my neck as Delia continues on with her announcements. Oddly, I feel shy and uncomfortable standing at the front of the room.

I'm no stranger to being in the spotlight. After every Eagles game, the school reporters come out to interview the team and take photos. Ironically, most of these game photos are taken by the very same person I'll be working with this summer. She might be the only one who doesn't make a big deal out of the Edendale Eagles.

Meanwhile, the rest of the reporters are shameless. As the reigning MVP, I'm top of the list for an interview and I've been well-groomed to answer their questions. If I'm honest, I don't feel I deserve the attention — my teammates are extremely talented players, many of them better than me. But, after every game, Lucas, Troy and I — the top striker, defender and midfielder — have microphones shoved into our faces from overeager student writers hoping to get a scoop.

My MVP status really hit home, though, when people

around Edendale began identifying me in the streets. It's a small enough town that people follow the Eagles throughout the year, and more than a few times, I've been approached by strangers asking for photos or commenting on my game.

The remoteness of Legacy Inn — located a 45-minute drive from Edendale — was definitely a perk.

Now, instead of feeling breezily confident, if not a little bored, I'm nervous standing at the front of the room. I remind myself why I'm here — to pursue something that I've never had the chance to pursue. My parents are way too overbearing during the year to give me the chance to practice my photography. Working here as a photographer was the perfect, safe option.

I glance down at my Fujifilm X-T4 and smile despite the rush of emotions. My grandad got me the camera a couple of years ago as a reward for my hard work at school. He was probably the only person who recognized that I'm more than just the star soccer player. In fact, he's the only one that I shared this part of my life with.

After what happened last fall, I shoved the camera into the back of my closet. But, when grandad passed away in the spring, I dug it back out. He always told me to do what I loved and his words are part of the reason I called the Inn on the off-chance they had a position as a photographer.

I glance down the line of students as Delia rambles on. To my relief, none of them look shocked or surprised or confused. In my mind, I could picture their outbursts.

"Jonathan, what are you thinking?"

"You're here to take photos? Hilarious!"

"You're a soccer player, stick to what you're good at."

My tense shoulders fall as I register their smiling, or bored, faces. Maybe they don't care.

There's only one grimace, and it comes from the person next to me. I can hear icicles forming around her. Everyone I've spoken with tonight is kind and welcoming, and their warmth is strongly contrasted with the chilly breeze emanating from Kiara.

A feeling of discomfort tugs at me and I finger the buttons on my camera absentmindedly. Over the years, we've taken shots at each other whenever we get the chance, but I have no clue how she will react to this news. I keep looking at her to make sure she isn't having a stroke.

Finally, Delia steps off the stage. I turn towards Kiara, but before I can extend an olive branch, she stalks off.

So that's how it's going to be.

The crowd disperses into smaller groups, all happily chattering away.

"Congrats, Jonathan!"

I turn around to face Bree, one of the students from Edendale. She hangs out with the Eagles on occasion, but doesn't seem particularly tied to any clique at school.

"Thanks, Bree."

"I thought you were here to teach the kids soccer or something. This is *not* what I expected."

I chuckle, grasping my camera. "Maybe next year."

Bree laughs and we head for the food table talking about the Inn. My stomach rumbles as one of the staff sets out a new plate of cheese bread, salami, and other appetizers. Any tension I was carrying melts away. Maybe my schoolmates won't be quite as discouraging as I feared.

Most of them, anyway.

12

KIARA

*H*ow did I not know about this?

I follow Delia's colorful dress through the crowd, trying to catch her. I didn't hear a word of her speech after she announced that Jonathan and I will both be photographers this summer. I couldn't move a muscle and my mouth dried up. I saw him shoot a few glances in my direction, but I was frozen.

As soon as Delia left the stage, he turned to talk to me, but I had no time for his words. He was probably going to say something snide anyway, and I have much more pressing matters.

Delia heads towards the DJ booth.

I cut her off. I need answers. Now.

"Uh, Delia?" I ask, my voice more hesitant than I intend.

Delia spins, an enormous smile on her face. "It's a lovely party, isn't it?"

"I think some wires were crossed."

"How so, my dear?" Delia fiddles with her cowboy hat and waves distractedly at people across the room.

"I was told I would be the *only* student photographer at

the Inn this summer."

Delia nods her head and focuses on me, grabbing my hand. "Ah yes. We've been busy with the Welcome Bash. Your friend was a last-minute hire. I bet you're excited to have him here!"

Friend?

"He called a few days ago," Delia says, either not noticing or completely ignoring the disappointed expression on my face. "And I thought, wouldn't that just be perfect? We've been wanting to take new photos of the Inn, and this way you don't have the burden of doing it all yourself."

I stand straight and force a smile. "It's definitely not a burden for me. I plan to become a photographer once I'm finished high school. This is exactly the sort of task I—"

"You sound so professional already!" Delia laughs. "There's time for work when you're older. When you're an adult."

"But—"

Delia gestures wildly across the room, almost swatting some unsuspecting staff member in the face. "You should be having fun! Work, yes, but we don't want you miserable while you're here. The Inn is a place to work, but it's also a place to play."

It's nothing I haven't heard before, and as always, the words bother me. People are always telling me that — I'm *young*, I should have *fun*. But there's no time for that, not when I have a prime opportunity on my hands. I can have fun once I'm successful.

Delia then stands straight, looking around. "And look at that, fate intervenes once again!"

To my horror, she grabs Jonathan's wrist as he walks through the crowd. He and one of the Edendale students —

Bree, I believe — are cutting across the room with plates piled high with food.

Delia grabs the plate from Jonathan and hands it to Bree. Grief flitters across his face as he watches his beloved food disappear.

"I bet you're excited to get to work with a friend from school," Delia says. "And I want you both to enjoy yourselves, to really let loose. This is a night of celebration. So dance together and have fun!"

Delia pushes us together and I raise my hands to stop us bumping into each other. In one seamless movement, Jonathan grabs my hands and starts doing an awkward jig. Not bothering to look at the car accident she just caused, Delia floats away, carrying Bree off to places unknown.

"Did you hear that? She said the 'F' word." Jonathan leans in. "Fun. Are queens even allowed to have fun?"

Jonathan is surprisingly light on his feet, but I'm no slouch. I match him step for step. "You dance well," I say. "Must be hard to balance with your extremely big head."

Without warning, Jonathan spins me, and just before I crash into the couple dancing next to us, he pulls me back into his arms. "Would you look at that? I saved you again."

I glare as he takes my other hand. There's an insane friction between our palms, threatening to push us far apart as soon as the song is over.

"Always the hero," I say sarcastically. "So, I have a question I'm just dying to ask."

"Look, if you're asking me out—"

"No," I say immediately. "Never that."

"Too bad. In the right light, you're almost cute."

I keep my expression neutral. "I'm just wondering how it feels to not be attached to a soccer ball? Disorienting? Lonely, perhaps?"

I see what I think is a hint of a smile, but before his face breaks, he dips me. He drops me so low to the ground it feels like I'm falling. "If I didn't know better, I'd say the Queen feels threatened. Her throne of photography is being challenged by a humble commoner."

I snort. It's decidedly unfeminine.

Not that I care how feminine Jonathan thinks I am.

"You're not humble, golden boy," I snap. "And threatened? By you? You wouldn't last a day working as my assistant."

Jonathan spins me again. This time, he sends me careening into the food table —

And then pulls me back just before I take flight over the appetizers.

"Didn't think a Queen would need an assistant," he says.

I'm close to him now, one of my hands resting on his surprisingly strong shoulder. "Assistants are the best part about being a queen," I say. "Do you know what the second-best part is?"

His hand slides over my hip and onto my lower back. "What's that?"

"When your assistant can't keep up, you get to take their head." I stare deep into his eyes. "But don't worry. I'll let you live."

The music slows and he pulls me close. Our footsteps mirror each other. We're surprisingly in sync for two people who hate each other so much.

"Don't take it easy on me, Your Majesty." His voice is low. "I think you'll find I'm quite the competitor."

We stare into each other's eyes, both refusing to look away as the world stops around us.

Whoever breaks first, loses.

And there's no way I'm letting Jonathan break me.

13

KIARA

*T*here's a loud shatter as someone accidentally drops a plate.

Jonathan and I look towards the crashing at the same moment.

He releases me, and without a second glance, heads towards the tables where the Edendale students are devouring appys. "See you around."

Everyone mingles, enjoying themselves. Music pumps through the speakers, people dance and laugh. I stand silently in the middle of the floor, still shaking off whatever just happened with Jonathan.

What was that crazy feeling?

Did he feel it too?

No. Couldn't be anything. Just hunger, probably.

I meander to the food table and load a plate with Chef Fernando's mac and cheese bites, some veggies, and a piece of lasagna before heading to an almost-empty table. Almost empty, except for Bree.

"Mind if I sit?"

"It's a free country," Bree says, not unkindly.

I take a seat and attack my lasagna with the ferocity of a starving coyote. I'm shoving the pasta in my mouth so fast that I'm probably wearing tomato sauce as lipstick, but I don't care.

"Kiara, right?" Bree asks, looking decidedly bored. "What do you think of the Inn so far?"

I shrug, wiping my face with a napkin. "Cabin's cute, bugs aren't bad, Delia's a character."

"That's putting it lightly," Bree says, chuckling. She looks out over the room, her next words an afterthought. "I don't know where my parents found her, but she's sure made a difference. They don't talk about it much, but we were struggling for a bit before she came along."

Bree's parents own the Inn. From what I've heard, they're flashy people, often on the road promoting the Inn or one of their other businesses.

Bree and I don't talk much at school. While I'm usually hanging out with the artsy kids, Bree floats from group to group, getting along with everyone. With her rose-gold hair and bright blue eyes, she's effortlessly beautiful. And she's got a wild streak — I've heard she's skipped school almost as much as she's attended — but she's able to charm her way into or out of most situations pretty easily.

Now, she seems distracted, looking around the room indignantly. We exchange a couple more words and then fall into a comfortable silence, which suits me as I'm too busy sulking.

This job was everything to me, the perfect summer opportunity to build up my portfolio for next year. And now, I just feel trapped and hopeless, thanks to fricking Jonathan.

Even a mountain of cheesy pasta can't improve my mood. I capture another few shots of the group having a good time, then leave.

I follow the path back towards the cabins, my distress transforming into stubborn determination. So Jonathan and I will both be photographers this summer. That doesn't mean we have to work closely together. If anything, it's an opportunity to shine, to showcase my skills compared to someone who has no clue what he's doing. Maybe this will push me to work harder, to take the best possible photos here at the Inn.

It's pitch black when I reach our little cabin community. The lights from the gravel path cast shadows across the area, and the cabin windows are dark. The hulking, black shapes look haunted in the darkness. Anything could be hiding here.

I shiver, then immediately chide myself for playing on childhood fears of the dark.

Still...

They are creepy.

I climb the steps to my cabin and the wood creaks under my foot.

Suddenly, something large scurries out from around the corner of my cabin.

I shriek.

It's a bear!

No.

It's a...

It's a...

It's a Jonathan.

I swear so loud that people on the other side of the state cover their ears.

Of course he's here. Why couldn't I have a little time to myself? A little time away from him?

Jonathan makes a face and rubs his ear. "Way to deafen the entire Inn, Garcia."

I'm both relieved and angry that he's not a bear. Relieved, because of obvious reasons. Angry, because it would've been better to be eaten by a bear than scared by Jonathan.

I put my hands on my hips. "Well, if *someone* wasn't so busy sneaking around our cabins at night, I wouldn't *need* to deafen anyone. What're you doing anyway? Checking to make sure your precious soccer jersey isn't being ruined by the fresh mountain air?"

Jonathan rolls his eyes so dramatically that I can see the move through the darkness.

"It's not really any of your business, is it?" He hops up the steps to his cabin, located next to mine. *Of course.* Delia's done an excellent job throwing Jonathan into my life at every opportunity.

His voice is mocking. "So we get to be photo buddies this summer. Should be fun. Maybe I can show you a thing or two?"

Is he joking? My anger flares up again as I face him head on.

"Listen here, golden boy. I am here for one reason and one reason only. I'm building up my portfolio so I can get out of that stinking pile of a town as soon as we graduate next year. I need this job for my future and nothing will distract me from that. Including your snide remarks, immature comments, and stupid questions."

I climb the steps to my cabin, finishing with: "Stay out of my way this summer, and we'll get along just fine."

With that, I turn on my heel and slam the door shut behind me.

My heart is racing and I'm out of breath. He may have hurt me long ago, but I won't let him get to me now.

Not again.

14

JONATHAN

*K*iara the Queen slams the door, retreating to her throne room.

Someone's having a bad day.

Unbeknownst to Kiara, I came back to my cabin to put my camera away after devouring about a thousand mac and cheese bites. I also wanted some fresh air after the intense moment we shared when dancing. Of course, Delia *would* pick me out in a crowd to throw us together.

Kiara has this unnerving way of seeing through me, like she knows something about me that I don't even know myself. During the dance, I wanted her to feel as uncomfortable as she makes me feel. I taunted her. Teased her. Spun her dangerously close to both people and food. But she gave everything back and more; completely unshakeable.

Then our eyes met and something indescribable shot through me.

I brush off the memory. When I got back here, I was going to crawl under her cabin to grab the soccer ball when I noticed that one window was slightly open. I shut it from the outside to keep the bugs out, and that's when her shriek almost killed me.

If I'd known it was her cabin, I would've opened the window wider.

Our rivalry goes too far back, the roots are too deep, for me not to mess with her a little.

I smile and follow the path back towards the Inn. It's not surprising that Kiara's only here to make progress towards her future. She's always had a one-track mind.

And it's paid off, hasn't it? She's a talented photographer, her skills are miles ahead of what I could ever hope to accomplish. I told her I was a great competitor, but deep down I know that next to her, I'll look like a complete fraud.

"Can I do this?" I ask the sky for what feels like the millionth time today. And for the millionth time, the sky doesn't have an answer.

The lights from the Inn get closer, and the happy chatter and laughter get louder. This is what I want. Working here at the Inn this summer feels right. But whether I have the skills and ability to be a photographer? To be determined.

Should I give up? Maybe I should just go to Momentum — scratch this whole photography thing and go back to soccer.

It isn't too late. I can hop on a bus tonight and get to Momentum by midday tomorrow. I can live the life my parents have so carefully planned out for me. I called the camp a couple of days ago to let them know I wouldn't be coming. They sounded surprised. Surely they'd take me if I showed up just a day late?

I kick a stone and watch it bounce into the darkness. That *is* what everyone wants and expects of me. My parents and closest friends think I'm already there. I can go back to being "Star Midfielder" and "MVP". The boy who's the "best" at everything. The one everyone is counting on to go to a big college on a full-ride soccer scholarship.

Funny enough, Kiara might be the only person in my life *without* these expectations of me. My family and friends, even strangers in the street, all expect the best of me. Kiara is the one person who doesn't. If anything, she blatantly believes I *can't* do it. She's set the bar so low, it's lying on the ground.

I blow out a puff of air, like I've been holding my breath for far too long. An odd sense of freedom and relaxation sweeps through me as I consider staying here.

The music is loud, and people are laughing on the balcony above me.

I close my eyes and smile. It feels like my first genuine smile in a very long time.

If I'm not the best here, will anyone care?

15

KIARA

*W*arm sunlight streams through the windows and the birds chirp outside. This is what it must feel like to be a princess in a fairy tale. I stretch out in my bed, pleasantly surprised by the good night's sleep.

This princess has to roll up her sleeves and get to work.

I hop out of bed and throw on my jean shorts and a top. I tie my wavy hair into a messy bun, pulling out a few strands to frame my face in an attempt to look "classy". After applying copious amounts of sunscreen and bug spray, I stroll over to the Inn for breakfast.

The guests arrive today, with the first expected in just a few minutes.

I find my way to the event room, which is buzzing with energy. Delia and Vin stand in the midst of the chaos. Delia is animatedly tapping her clipboard and adjusting her cowboy hat while Vin gestures about the room.

I'm about to ask where I can get breakfast when I spot a few staffers filing out of a door at the far end of the room. Dodging the chairs and tables set up all around, I head over and find a sign labeled "Staff Room".

A smile crosses my face as I enter. Big windows fill one wall of the staff room and there are several tables and chairs set up for meals. In one corner, a couple of old couches and shelves with various books and board games invite people to sit back and relax. "Only on their breaks, of course!" I imagine in Delia's voice.

"Good morning!" Fernando's voice booms behind me as he enters from what I assume is the kitchen. "You're Kiara — one of the photographers?"

"What gave me away?" I smile and tap my camera. Fernando's a large, cheery man with a big smile and light eyes. His dark hair is tied into a bun under his chef's hat.

Fernando laughs.

Noah, one of the Edendale High kids, walks into the room. He heads for the food table, clearing up some empty trays. Noah is one of those kids that everyone knows about, but no one actually knows. I've heard he has like 2 part-time jobs during the year aside from his schoolwork. Despite being the school's mystery guy, he's always happy to lend a hand.

"You'd better get your breakfast quick. Noah's on a mission this morning." Fernando gives Noah a wink. Noah, with a bagel clenched between his teeth, smiles and ducks out with the empty trays.

"Looks like a couple of bagels survived his mission," I say. The food table is filled with amazing options, but there's something missing. I keep my voice quiet, not wanting to impose. "Do you happen to have any avocado?"

Fernando turns around and marches back into the kitchen. I stand for a moment, wondering if my avocado request might've somehow insulted his innate chef-ness. He returns and hands me a perfectly ripe avocado. "I've never tried avocado on a bagel before."

I grab a bagel. "Let me make one for you, it's my favorite."

Fernando shows me into the kitchen and I put together his bagel with cream cheese, avocado, and tomato. It's a staple for weekends when my mom is at work and we happen to have an avocado in the house.

After sprinkling salt and pepper on top, I pass the plate to Fernando. He takes a big bite and smiles.

"Wonderful. We might need to add this to the menu for the season," he says.

My cheeks flush red. I enjoy cooking and trying out new recipes — if we have any ingredients in the house. But to have something I made — however simple — complimented by a chef? That's something I never would have expected.

"You know where to find me if you need the recipe," I say, winking, before I make up my own bagel. "Thanks Fernando!"

I follow the buzz of energy out of the Inn and into the garden, happy to see that I'm getting better at finding my way through this place. I take another bite of my bagel and head to the lake. It's the perfect spot to wait for guests.

The lake is astonishingly beautiful this morning. Little ripples travel over the surface so the reflection of the mountains seems alive. I finish my bagel and snap a few shots. One of these is sure to work for the Glacier Journal.

Finally, the guests start arriving, and I give them my full attention. I capture the joy and excitement in their faces as they see the Inn for the first time. I get the wonder in their eyes when they spot the lake. There's a lively, dynamic atmosphere and I can't keep the smile off my face.

Until Jonathan comes wandering down the path.

He's late. He probably spent last night partying instead

of taking this assignment seriously. And why would he take it seriously? He probably has some fancy internship he can fall back on if he needs it. Not that it's any of my business, as he so kindly pointed out.

"Little late to the game, golden boy? I hope we didn't disturb your beauty sleep," I say as he gets closer.

Jonathan rolls his eyes in response, standing a few feet away from me.

His hair is wet from the shower and he's wearing a loose hoodie and shorts. I've rarely seen him without his soccer gear or his polo shirts. As he takes out his camera and scrambles to put it on, a strange feeling comes over me. I've never seen Jonathan look uncertain or vulnerable. It's weirdly... cute.

What are you thinking, Kiara?

I shake myself off and focus on the guests as they set up around the area. I feel a bit sorry for him. He's struggling to get his camera ready, and he seems stressed.

Could it be? Does Jonathan actually *care* about doing a good job at Legacy Inn?

16

JONATHAN

*K*iara watches as I fiddle with the buttons on my camera. Something about her makes me nervous.

My stomach grumbles and I clear my throat to cover it. I didn't have time for breakfast this morning. I took a shower in the bathroom block by the cabins and the water was ice cold. It took me a while to properly wash off, and I had to run straight here afterwards.

"First time with a camera, golden boy?" Kiara asks.

I glare and adjust the settings on my camera.

At school, we fall into our rivalry effortlessly. Most of the time, we're able to avoid each other. And when we do see each other, either in class or at the end of an Eagles match, one of us lobs a snarky comment and the other claps back.

Part of me has come to enjoy our banter over the years. She's the only girl at school who doesn't seem completely blinded by the fact that I play for the Eagles.

Finally, I start snapping photos. I get a couple of shots of the lake before turning towards the guests, but my mind wanders to my ex-girlfriend, Isabella.

When we were dating, the whole "status" thing got old quickly. We started dating in our sophomore year, right before I gained the "star midfielder" label. She was gunning for head cheerleader but, when she got it, everything changed. It was very important to her that I boast about my status, given her prestigious position. When she broke up with me to date another top athlete this past spring, I was relieved.

I dated a couple of girls after, but nothing serious. All the conversations eventually centered on my being a state champion player, and how that could get us into the hottest parties and clubs in Edendale. It only got worse after we won the state championship two years in a row and I was awarded MVP.

That's when I lost interest in partying. After one too many pointless conversations about how great it must be to be the "star soccer kid" at Edendale High, I stopped going to the parties. No one understood the pressure I was under, and certainly no one wanted to talk about it.

I line up the camera to take a shot of the newcomers and begrudgingly realize that Kiara was right to choose this spot. Standing here by the lake offers a perfect vantage point to get the expressions on guests' faces as they arrive.

But something isn't working. I check back over the photos and frown. The images are dark, colorless, like they're missing something.

"Try moving closer to the dock. The sunlight hits the water and gives their faces a glow. Think of the lake as a giant reflector board." Kiara's smug voice floats over to me and I look up in surprise. The Queen strikes again. Her wide brown eyes are patronizing and she has a slightly disdainful look on her face. As usual, she comes across condescending.

But I guess she *does* have more experience than I do...

Without a word, I move closer to the dock and snap another photo of the elderly couple sitting on chairs in the garden. I look at the photo and the difference is night and day.

The photo looks clean, crisp and professional. I smile.

I glance up and catch a cute half-smile on Kiara's face before she quickly drops the smile and goes back to looking displeased.

"Thanks." Whether or not she did it to be nice, her advice helped.

She smirks, her eyes boring into mine.

I hold her gaze for a moment and something strange happens. A wave passes between us. But then, she looks away, and the moment is gone.

17

KIARA

"*D*id you hear? Kade Monroe is spending the entire summer here. He's filming a new movie in the National Park." Nath's voice is a whisper of excitement.

I've come inside for a glass of water and have stopped to chat with Nath. She's the landscape architect here at the Inn, and I wanted to know how she gets her inspiration. The garden looks spectacular this evening, as many of the guests have pointed out.

After explaining the intricacies of growing wisteria on outdoor arches, she turned her attention to the subject that was currently thrilling the Inn workers.

"Kade Monroe..." The name is vaguely familiar. "The guy from those action movies?"

"They're only the *best* action movies!" Nath exclaims and then raises her eyebrows up and down. "Vin watches for the thrill, I watch for Kade."

I laugh at Nath's starstruck expression, and she lowers her voice once again. "He and his son, Cooper, are both staying here in the penthouse at the far end of the property."

I stifle another laugh as Nath looks off dreamily into the distance. I'm not one to get starstruck around famous people, but Nath sounds like quite the fan. She squeezes my hand as Delia calls out from the reception.

"Kiara, they need you by the garden!"

Per Delia's instructions, I head downstairs to work. It's a beautiful evening, the perfect first night of vacation for many of the guests. The low buzz of cheerful conversation and laughter are intoxicating and I'm enjoying the aura of relaxation.

On the porch, a couple has commandeered one of the porch swings and they're laughing and chatting. I ask to take their photo and they happily oblige.

I thread my way through the crowd of people in the garden. Fairy lights glow from the trees, and cute colored lanterns line the stone walkways leading to white tables and garden chairs. People bustle at the outdoor bar, getting their drinks and snacks. An early summer breeze carries the scent of roses and lavender. Overhead, the sky is a muted pink as the sun sets behind the peaks. I've never seen anything like it.

As I stroll through the crowd, I'm thankful for the little black dress I packed. I even brushed my hair into something of a cute updo, and I'm wearing a touch of mascara. My mom would categorically disapprove of such a display, but I'm surprised to find I actually like dressing up — at least a little.

It helps that everyone around me is dressed beautifully. The women wear bright, colorful dresses and skirts reminiscent of an international issue of Vogue. The men are wearing casual suits and slacks.

I spot Jonathan as I'm approaching the gate leading to

the lakeshore. Delia may have intended for the two of us to work together, but I've done a good job avoiding him.

Now, curiosity gets the best of me. What's he up to?

Jonathan leans against one of the tables by the dance floor, laughing hard. He is the picture of carefree, and he's charming the elderly lady he's speaking with. Naturally, the golden boy is out and about sweetening everyone up.

His dark jeans and white shirt fit him perfectly, showing off his soccer muscles. Tonight, his blond hair falls naturally across his forehead, not slicked in that gel guys use. He cleans up nicely — for a stuck-up soccer player.

Get it together, Kiara.

After our bizarre moment of eye contact by the lake, I quickly made an excuse to leave. I can't explain what came over me when his blue eyes met mine. It was an electric shock that stole my breath — something I definitely don't want to happen again.

I shake away the thought and I'm about to turn away when something makes me pause.

Jonathan places his camera on the table and holds out his hand to the elderly woman. She takes it, laughing, and he leads her to the dance floor. There's a fun, catchy song playing and he spins her around in circles, dipping her twice.

Her laughter is contagious and I can't stop a smile from spreading across my face as I watch them dance together. He's laughing too as she shows him a move or two.

I remember his hands guiding me in a dance last night. He sure knows how to have a good time.

He dips her a third time, and his eyes meet mine. Everything goes quiet. He smiles. It's not the smug, conceited smirk I'm used to. It's not the celebratory smile I've captured so often after he's scored a goal, either. This is something different. Something warm.

My legs are made of rubber, and it's amazing I don't fall when I take my next step. Breathless, I look away.

Seriously, Kiara. Get. It. Together.

I walk through the crowd without looking back, disappearing from his blue-eyed gaze.

18

KIARA

*I*t's not that Jonathan's a *bad* person, he's just... fake.

It's past midnight and I'm sitting on my bed scrolling through the photos I've taken this evening. The first garden party of the summer was an absolute blast, to my surprise. But my mind is long-gone, given to a memory.

Though Jonathan and I have never been close, the first blow was dealt a couple of years ago, back when we were freshmen. It was the first Eagles game of the season, and it was my first job as a photographer for the school newspaper.

It was Jonathan's first game — he was one of two freshmen on the varsity team. In elementary school, he was the quiet, dedicated soccer kid who got pulled out of school for training and who got everything he wanted from his doting parents. At Edendale High, he'd quickly become one of the up-and-coming players for the Eagles.

It didn't help that he'd transformed from awkward boy to teenage heartthrob virtually overnight. And me? Still mousy, clumsy, and insecure.

After the game, he was hanging out on the field with his teammates and the reporters for the school paper.

And I was late.

"Sorry!" I yelled as I caught up with the group.

The reporters — mostly seniors — rolled their eyes. They'd wrapped up their interviews, so the players were waiting for photos. A senior I didn't recognize pretended to tap an imaginary watch on his wrist.

Flustered, I set up my camera on a tripod, then called the Eagles to attention.

"Guys?" My voice was quiet. Photography was my passion, but I still felt shy and unsure of my abilities. "Sorry, would you mind just—"

"Jon, this is dope!"

A player pushed past me and almost knocked over my tripod. My camera was only a point-and-shoot, but it was still precious. I dove and caught it just before it crashed to the ground.

"Watch it, Lucas," Jonathan said. He raised an eyebrow and looked at me. "You good, photo girl?"

I blushed furiously and set my tripod back on its feet. My cheeks burned as all of the hot soccer players stared at the awkward girl with the camera — me.

"I'm fine." I cleared my throat.

Jonathan smiled. My heart nearly burst and my legs went numb. Remember, this was back when I still thought he was kind.

And that's when everything changed.

The soccer player who almost destroyed my camera, Lucas, was the only other freshman on the varsity team. And he was clearly the only one who knew who I was.

He turned to me and rolled his eyes. "Don't worry about her, Jon. She's just the photo chick. You'd think she'd make more of an effort to protect her camera, given that it's her one and only friend."

The seniors burst into laughter.

My cheeks flamed red, and I wished I could disappear.

My eyes met Jonathan's, and he sheepishly turned away, laughing quietly with the rest of the group. My voice had left me, and within moments, tears filled my eyes. I ran full-speed off of the field.

It took months for me to brave another Eagles game, but that moment changed me. From then on, I dove into my persona as a photographer. I took my mom's advice and shamelessly pursued my future. I was going to show them all — Lucas, Jonathan, everyone — that the "photo girl" would succeed.

Since then, I have had a singular goal — to get a job as a photographer and get out of town right after graduation.

As bad as that moment was, the aftermath was worse. Lucas became known around school for being a player and an all-around jerk. In a way, I didn't have a bone to pick with him — put simply, he's mean and doesn't hide it.

But Jonathan? He's worse.

He may not have said the words that broke my heart and made the entire team laugh at me, but he went along with the joke. That side of him is a betrayal — the side that laughs at the expense of others, that can't stand up for people when it matters the most. And yet, Jonathan is known around school for being "kind" and "nice". Edendale High's golden boy.

In the past, I've tried to explain my side of the story to friends of mine, but no one believed that Jonathan would *ever* behave that way.

No one but Ava. It's no surprise that we became friends.

And it goes further than that. I've heard he gets stopped

by strangers around Edendale, obliging their questions and photos. If you believed the rumors and town gossip, Jonathan Wright can do no wrong.

The only funny aspect, albeit morbidly so, is that he and his buddies think they're so smart. Lucas coined the oh-so-clever "Kiara the Queen" nickname last fall. But don't they know that calling me "Queen" demands respect?

The moon shines bright through my windows, and I switch off my camera with a sigh. The uncomfortable memory fills me with dread and determination, but this evening, I feel something else.

Seeing Jonathan struggle with his camera today was weirdly eye-opening.

In that moment, he wasn't the Edendale High golden boy, and he wasn't the jerk from the Eagles. He was just a guy, completely confused and out of his depths.

I remember meeting his gaze by the lake earlier, and when he danced with the elderly lady tonight at the garden party. That was a Jonathan Wright I don't know or recognize.

So who is he, really?

19

JONATHAN

"Oh, Jonathan!" Delia's sing-song voice reaches me from across the staff room.

I look up from the bagel I'm devouring. After missing breakfast yesterday and being ravenous until lunchtime, I'm not making the same mistake twice. Wes and I are eating together. Kiara is nowhere to be seen. Probably late, as usual.

Delia swoops across the room, her cowboy hat almost blowing off in the breeze of her stride.

"There you are!" She stops in front of our table.

"Gotta go," Wes blurts, dismissing himself before Delia can launch into her latest request.

Delia pats him on the shoulder as he takes off. "Don't forget your whistle, my boy."

Wes lifts his lifeguard whistle from under his shirt and salutes her. I stifle a snort. Delia means well, but she sure acts like a drill sergeant at times.

She turns her sparkling green gaze on me. "Jonathan, today is a perfect opportunity to get some gazebo photos. Kiara is there now, and I wanted to make sure you'll be headed there as well and not to the lake or the garden. Best to strike while the iron is hot!"

I scramble to my feet, downing my orange juice and the rest of my bagel in one gulp. "Already on my way."

"Good." She smiles. "Now, I need to find Noah. That boy works too hard. He volunteered this morning to help Fernando. Can you believe it?"

Delia's off before I can respond.

I grab my camera bag and head outside. My thoughts race, and my stomach churns the bagel and orange juice uneasily. The last time I felt this nervous, I was standing in the locker room before my first soccer game at Edendale.

Okay, day two, Jonathan, you can do this.

Kiara's challenge echoes in my mind. I told her I was quite the competitor, but would I actually be able to keep up? My heart sinks. It's only day two and I'm already behind.

"You got this, dude," I mumble to myself as I jog through the garden.

"Someone there?" A bush yells.

I jump with the grace of a startled cat. When I land, I see that no, obviously, the bush didn't yell. It was Nath.

I pretend to clutch my chest. "I think — I THINK — my heart is still beating."

Nath's sunhat pokes over a pink rosebush. She emerges and takes off her gloves. "Just keeping you on your toes. Vin calls me low-budget espresso. I'm good at waking people up and getting their hearts racing."

"Can't disagree with that."

Behind Nath, another person appears from the bush. The woman is in her late-30s and her black hair is cut in a bob. Her eyes are kind but sharp.

Nath turns towards the woman. "Randy, this is the kid I was telling you about — Jonathan."

Randy crosses her arms and smiles. "What's the soccer player doing with a camera?"

"It's a mystery to us all," Nath says in a stage whisper.

I laugh. I'm the furthest thing from a mystery. Except to myself, maybe.

"Nice to meet you, Jonathan." Randy smiles warmly and extends her hand. I shake it and can't believe how firm her grip is.

"You too. Anyway, I gotta go, duty calls."

I continue to the gazebo, picking up my pace. Warm sunlight bounces radiantly off the lake. I don't think anyone could ever get tired of a view like that.

Kiara's in the gazebo lining up a group for a photo.

I groan. She's going to give me a hard time. Again.

"Making a habit out of being late, golden boy?" She keeps her voice low so the subjects can't hear.

"Are photographers supposed to be on time? From seeing you at Eagles games, I thought that punctuality was optional."

She rolls her eyes dramatically and adjusts her XF 56mm lens. "I'm never late for people and things I actually *care* about."

My mind rolls through a handful of half-clever responses when she suddenly turns towards me, her face the mask of suspicious innocence. "Jonathan, why don't you take the photos here today?"

My jaw drops. Her voice is polite, professional, and just loud enough for the group in the gazebo to hear. She's trying to make me look like her assistant. Behind her, the group is shifting from foot to foot, waiting for us to get started.

"That's not a great idea," I stammer, trying desperately to

think of an excuse. "I don't know if that lens will fit my camera."

As soon as the words are out of my mouth, I regret them. Her face relaxes into a half-smile. She's got me and she knows it.

"Don't be silly. We have the same camera. And the same lenses."

Before I can even pretend to think of another excuse, she takes the lens off her camera and steps back. "Go on."

Dread falls over me like a weighted blanket. Yesterday was my first day attempting serious photography since last fall. In my cabin this morning, I practiced taking a few shots and switching out my lenses, but I still feel shaky. Add on to that the pressure of having Kiara and the guests watching me? It's a disaster waiting to happen.

Delia's words echo in my mind about striking while the iron's hot. What if I mess up this opportunity? I'd never hear the end of it from Delia. Or Kiara.

Can I risk it?

"Scared?" Kiara faces me so the guests can't see her conniving smile. "If you give up and admit defeat, I'll help you out. Teach you a thing or two."

Scared?

Give up?

That kicks my butt into gear. Sure, the photos I capture might not be perfect, but better to dive in and drown than admit defeat. I puff out my chest and stand up straight, striding confidently to the group in front of the gazebo.

"Okay, you two on the ends, I want you guys to move in."

I direct the group to rearrange themselves, placing the tallest people in the middle instead of the edges. I make a few more adjustments and tell one of the women to brush a stray hair from her face.

"That's a lot of confidence for someone who doesn't know what they're doing," Kiara says.

I won't let her get to me. "It's good that you're staying to watch. You might learn a thing or two yourself."

I fiddle with my own XF 56mm lens for a moment, struggling to get it on the camera. My palms are sweaty as the nerves take over. The pressure of Kiara's gaze isn't helping.

"Do you need a hand? We don't have all day, after all." Her voice is sweet as sugar. She leans casually against a tree, her arms crossed.

"Well, that's just not true," I say. I smile at the guests. "The beauty of a vacation at Legacy Inn is that we have all the time in the world."

The group chuckles and I know I've won this round.

A victorious smile crosses my face as the camera shutter clicks.

20

KIARA

"So... how does it feel to work with Edendale's star midfielder?"

Bree sets her plate down next to mine on the table. Across from us, Stefi and Anaya take their seats, and we all tuck into our breakfasts. As always, the chat turns to Jonathan.

"More and more of his goldenness is rubbing off on me every day? Can't you tell?" I bat my eyelashes like a cartoon princess.

Bree and Anaya snicker, and a smile crosses Stefi's face.

Just four days into our time at Legacy Inn, all of Edendale's rules have been broken. The four of us would never sit together at school. But Anaya joined us for breakfast yesterday and we've fallen into a good flow.

"I bet he knows exactly what he's doing, that one." Anaya smiles. With her long dark hair and gymnast's figure, Anaya was a shoo-in for cheerleader in her freshman year at Edendale High. She joined the squad and stayed through sophomore year, but she dropped out in junior year. She says she couldn't stand the drama that came with being a cheerleader.

"It's just—" I shove a piece of bagel into my mouth, pondering what I want to say. "He's got it all *so* easy. I can't imagine a world where Jonathan fails. And even if he fails, he's got a golden safety net."

"Ki. You know we love you—" Bree starts, putting her hand on my wrist.

"Love me? We only officially met like 72 hours ago."

She ignores my interruption. "You're taking all of this too seriously. It's time to let go. Relax. Maybe knock him off his pedestal a little or something."

Anaya and Stefi are both nodding at me, like wise owls.

Ugh. First Delia, now these guys. Why is everyone so obsessed with me enjoying myself this summer?

Anaya looks around conspiratorially, then leans in. "Guys, I need to ask your advice. It's Daniel. What do you think about..."

Anaya's voice fades into the distance. It would be nice to have a little fun this summer. Imagine, for just one second, being as carefree as Jonathan seems to be every single moment. Who says I can't get the job done while having a little fun on the side?

The thought of having fun is enough to recall the stern-faced image of my mom. She frowns and tells me to focus on my future.

My shoulders slump as I finish my breakfast. Fun? That's a pipe dream. Someday, when I'm successful, I'll come back here as a guest. Then I'll have more than enough fun for everyone.

After breakfast, we say our goodbyes and I head outside to find my absolute *favorite* person.

It doesn't take long to spot the golden boy, with his

matching golden hair, over by the gazebo. I puff out my cheeks and exhale in a huff.

Another day of working with Jonathan Wright. Ever since he vowed to keep up with me, I've been throwing challenge after challenge his way. I've put on the pressure, given him a hard time, and left him with difficult tasks.

Tasks he shouldn't be able to accomplish.

But he's keeping up.

Which means I need to try harder to throw him off.

I would never admit it, but I'm actually impressed by how dedicated he's been to photography. Ever since the Welcome Bash, he's held his own. Even when he's fumbling with lenses, you can tell he's putting in an honest effort.

And as for his natural charm? That makes my job a lot easier.

"Yo, golden boy," I call out as I approach Jonathan.

He turns, a halo of sunlight behind him. I shake my head, confused, until I realize that the light is reflecting off the lake water. He literally looks like he's glowing.

I jog over to escape the trick of the light, and I'm surprised to see he's wearing a hoodie with his board shorts. I don't hate the look, especially because he looks *so* much less pretentious than he does in his polo shirts.

"How much damage have you done this morning?" I ask as he fiddles with one of his lenses.

"Hmm, must be hard," he says, not bothering to meet my eyes.

"What?"

"Just like, being so *on* all the time." He finally looks at me with a passive gaze. "It's exhausting just listening to your voice."

I place my hand on my hip and raise my eyebrows. "Fortunately for you, only one of us needs to be *on* to do this job right. Why don't you play with your little soccer ball or whatever?"

"I can't. It's wedged under your cabin." A slight smile crosses his face. "Come on, Kiara the Queen. You *know* you're allowed to have fun, right?"

That is it! My cheeks turn bright red and I finally explode.

"What is with everyone? *Why* is everyone ragging on me to have fun? What's the deal?!"

I glare at Jonathan, waiting for him to give me an answer. To my satisfaction, he looks taken aback. Serves him right.

"You know you're more than just your work, right?"

His words send weird goosebumps over my skin. I open my mouth to retort, but nothing comes out. My throat is dry and, for once, I'm speechless.

A group of guests approaches from the Inn, snapping me out of the moment. Everyone wants photos at the gazebo, and we've gotten used to the morning rush.

But even as guest after guest passes by in a blur, Jonathan's words echo through my mind.

I'm more than just my work?

21

KIARA

"Say Legacy!" I call out to the two girls standing on the dock.

Click. The camera captures the shot, and I check it out on the screen. But something isn't right.

I glance towards my subjects. The twins can't be more than 5 or 6 years old, and they won't stop moving around. In fact, the issue is that the girl on the right is less of a girl and more of a blur.

"Mom, can we play in the lake yet?" The girl on the left calls out, drawing out the "o".

The twins' mother stands to the side, speaking in hushed tones to her husband. Upon hearing her daughter's voice, she whips around, her short, carefully coiffed hair barely moving.

"Not until we get the shot." She turns to me. "You. Photo girl. Did you get it or not?"

Photo girl?

Seriously?

Most of the Inn's guests are charming, but this woman

makes me want to throw something into the lake. Maybe her.

"Uh…" I look at the photo again. I want to set the girls free. They're both tugging at their dresses and shifting from foot to foot, staring at the lake wistfully. I understand their pain.

Unfortunately, my answer doesn't come fast enough.

"Girls. Stop. Moving." She orders and the girls both sigh dramatically. "Take *one* good photo for your dad and then you can do whatever you want."

The woman whips back around to continue her conversation and the girls cross their arms, glaring at the camera. Clearly, they want to be here as much as I do.

"Okay, kids." My voice is small as I paste on a friendly smile. "Just one more and then you're free to go to the lake."

My words do little to change their attitudes. They both have perfectly sour looks on their faces and I frown, trying to think of a good way to cheer them up.

"Hey kids, check this out." The voice belongs to Jonathan.

The girls' frowns disappear.

Their eyes go wide.

And a slow-motion montage of terror plays out.

First, something light lands on my head. Something with distinct, pointy legs.

Next, my hand slams down on the top of my head and my fingers contact a fuzzy, round, fat creature.

I shriek so loud the mountains wince.

"Get it off! Get it off!"

I dance around, trying to get the *thing* off of me. Where is it? Did I get it? Is it dead? Is it caught in my hair? Please, oh please, let it not be a spider!

After a hectic storm of movement, I slow down, realizing the creature — whatever it was — no longer appears to be on my body.

What the?

I stand straight and look around me wildly, my hair flying around my face and my loose T-shirt crumpled around my torso.

Jonathan has the biggest grin I've ever seen. He's looking through his camera, taking photos of the twin girls who are now cracking up. Their laughter and smiles are infectious. Jonathan's getting every single moment of it.

If steam could come from my ears, I could power a frickin' steam boat.

My cheeks turn bright red as I spot the girls' mother, and a bunch of other guests, staring my way, completely shell-shocked. The silence is deafening, save for the laughter.

"Sorry, all," I manage, smiling sheepishly. "False alarm."

After a few hesitant moments, the happy chatter returns. Whispers and mumblings travel through the crowd, and the occasional guest looks my way. My face will be permanently red with embarrassment after this debacle.

As soon as the girls hurry away to jump into the lake, I march over to Jonathan and smack him on the arm.

"What was that?!"

"What?" His face is the picture of innocence.

"You know what! Why did you do that?"

Then, from behind his back, Jonathan pulls out the *creature*. It's a spider with eight spindly legs, eight black eyes, and an abdomen the size of a walnut. It's also made of rubber.

His eyes are wet and he can barely breathe.

IS HE SERIOUSLY LAUGHING SO HARD HE'S CRYING?

He's able to contain his laughter just long enough to get out a single sentence:

"Long... live... the queen."

22

JONATHAN

*I*f I could whistle, I really would.

Kiara's expression when I pranked her with the fake spider was immensely satisfying. Looking into her eyes was like looking into a raging bonfire. And her face? Even tomatoes don't get that red.

I stroll down the path towards the Inn, looking through my photos. The guests have all gone in for lunch and it's our staff lunchtime too. There's a great photo of the twins hugging each other and jumping up and down while they laugh.

It's perfect.

On top of trying to keep up with Kiara this week, we're in a side war to see who can get the most photos posted to the Inn's social media accounts. Kiara is currently winning — all the photos posted so far have been hers — but one of these might just do the trick.

I need to show Delia soon. I make a mental note to catch up with her once the day is done. I have a feeling one of these photos will be the winner today.

I catch up with Noah and Wes in the staff room, taking a

seat by the windows. I let them in on the prank I pulled on Kiara and they both burst into laughter.

"I can't believe you did that, and in front of the guests." Noah laughs, giving me a fist bump. "Kudos, bro."

"Anaya was saying that Kiara *hates* bugs. I'm sure that was real fun for her," Wes pipes in quietly, a smile on his face.

Fernando is serving up sandwiches today and I dig into mine hungrily, chomping through it in two bites. Wes and Noah both stare and I shrug.

"Pranking people really takes it out of you."

We finish our lunches and are about to grab some Oreo cookies before returning to work when none other than Kiara Garcia approaches our table. To my surprise, she looks vulnerable, staring down at the floor.

I've never seen anyone look so defeated.

"Golden boy," she says, a resigned look on her face. She has the energy of a neglected puppy. "I wanted to apologize. You were right. I do need to have some fun."

This is a surprise. I sit straight in my chair, waiting for her to continue. It's brave to apologize like this in front of Wes and Noah.

"Seeing you laughing and joking around with those kids opened my eyes to something. Sure, the Inn is a place to work. But it's also a place to play."

She lifts her face, and her eyes meet mine. She looks so sincere, so genuine, and I soften to her words. Are we really laying down our weapons? Is Kiara the Queen holding up a white flag?

"So I'm sorry. I'm hoping we can be friends."

I blink a few times to make sure this is reality and not, in fact, a dream.

"You serious?" I want to believe her. It is Kiara the Queen I'm talking to, but she looks so... sad.

"Very serious."

I nod slowly. Is our rivalry over? Can I forgive her for what she did last fall? I look her up and down, trying to assess whether I'm ready for our rivalry to end.

Kiara's eyes are gentle and kind, I've never seen her so vulnerable.

"So, friends?" she asks, holding out an Oreo.

I look into her eyes once again. After everything that's happened between us, can we really be friends?

I'd like to try.

I smile gratefully and take the Oreo, accepting her peace offering. Without taking my eyes from hers, I bite into the cookie.

There's a satisfying chocolate cookie crunch.

And then there's...

There's...

A blast of horribly intense mint.

I cough and chunks of cookie fly onto the table. I try to talk, but the horrible mint taste makes it impossible to do anything but cough.

Kiara's face transforms. A wicked half-smile comes across her lips and her eyes sparkle in devilish joy. Behind her, Anaya, Stefi and Bree are cracking up. So are Wes and Noah.

"It's a new flavor of Oreo," Kiara says, backing away as I cough again. "I believe it's called Crest Extra Whitening?"

The potent, overpowering minty taste of toothpaste fills my mouth. She replaced the icing with toothpaste.

Kiara curtsies in front of everyone watching, and the traitors all applaud.

She grins at me. "As you said, Jonathan. Long live the Queen."

I try to respond, but instead of a scathing comeback, I cough out a piece of Crest Extra Whitening Oreo.

This.

Means.

War.

23

KIARA

"Girl, that was crazy!" Bree says as we hurry out of the staff room. Stefi and Anaya have already rushed back to work.

"It was all you! You were my inspiration," I say. My stomach hurts from laughter.

Bree hushes away the compliment. Always so modest.

"Okay, but seriously," she says. We descend to the garden. "What's next? What's your master plan?"

I stroke a pretend beard and gaze out over to the lake. "I have a few things planned — assuming that golden boy doesn't immediately wave the white flag of surrender. I have a feeling he's got a couple pranks lined up himself, so I'm going to lie low. But when he strikes, I'll come back even harder."

Bree and I snicker wickedly, plotting his demise.

"Garcia." A familiar voice calls and Bree and I jump apart. Speak of the devil.

"Nice move." Jonathan says, brushing his hair out of his eyes. He's got a tiny speck of white at the corner of his mouth and some absurd part of me wants to wipe it off.

"I'll accept your surrender now, if you want," I say, smirking.

He leans in close. So close I can smell his aftershave. He whispers, his breath warm against my ear. "You're right, you know. I do have a couple things lined up for you."

I hold my breath, frozen. He's so close, his chest is almost touching mine.

"Sleep with one eye open." He straightens and steps out of the garden, looking back at me and gesturing with two fingers to say, "I'm watching you."

"Dude's intense." Bree's voice breaks the spell. She squeezes my arm. "See ya later, Ki. I gotta get back."

I'm still standing there in the garden a moment later, holding my camera. Something very weird is happening. Some familiar, but entirely unwelcome, stirring is happening in my stomach. Dare I say... a lone butterfly?

No. Kiara, no. You're being ridiculous. Jonathan Wright does *not* give you butterflies, just a case of mild nausea.

Ugh. I roll my eyes and breathe through the sensation. No point in dwelling on it.

I turn and skip out of the garden, trying to regain the happy feeling I had but moments ago.

24

JONATHAN

A musical tone intertwines with my dream, and I come rushing out of my peaceful sleep. My alarm might be on its quietest setting, but it feels like it's blaring.

"Rawwg!" I grunt as I hit snooze. I roll over, blinking my tired eyes open. "I thought I'd have a break from this over the summer."

It's 5:30am, and the world is just waking up. In a matter of minutes, I'll be wide awake and ready to go — my body has been trained to fare well with early mornings. But I'm not used to doing early mornings in combination with late nights.

It's been a week since I arrived at Legacy Inn and the last few days have been hectic. To keep up with Kiara, I've been staying awake with the last of the guests, hanging around in the evenings to take advantage of any photo ops. But, in keeping with Kiara's crazy schedule, I've also been up early a few times to capture the guests' sunrise paddles or breakfasts in the garden.

It's exhausting. Kiara could give my coach a run for his money.

I'd never tell her this, but I admire her dedication. She's so intensely committed to photography. She's not at all afraid to be honest and open about her dream. She's just unapologetically... herself.

I walk out to the bathroom block to brush my teeth, looking for light over the horizon. It'll be sunrise soon, my chance to capture the next photo for the Inn's social media accounts.

I've had fun this week competing with Kiara to get the most photos posted on social media. She's two photos ahead of me, so the photo posted today needs to be one of mine.

I look in the bathroom mirror, rub my hands over my stubble — there's been no time to shave — and smile.

Kiara is unlike any girl I've known. She roasts me almost as badly as Troy does, but it always makes me laugh. Her face breaks into this cute little half-smile when she thinks she's really got me. And she's so witty, her intelligence challenges me.

So, as you'd expect, our pranks this week have only escalated.

After her prank with the cookie, I knew I had to hit back harder — and fast. I hijacked one of her morning bagels and put a healthy layer of horseradish under her cream cheese. She took a big bite and her face practically glowed from the heat.

Meanwhile, I almost fell off my chair laughing.

Her retaliation came sooner than expected. That same evening, I returned from the garden party, opened my door, and there was a loud blare that gave me a minor heart attack. I checked behind my cabin door, and sure enough, she had rigged an air horn so that it would sound off when the door opened. Once my hearing returned, all I could hear was Kiara's incessant snickering from her tiny balcony.

Stefi and Cooper Monroe, son of the famous actor Kade Monroe, aided my next prank. They passed along a stack of his dad's headshots, and while Kiara was out taking photos, I strategically covered her entire cabin with them. The shot was perfect, too — it was Kade Monroe, topless, carrying an anaconda over his shoulders, with a look of pure intensity on his face.

I lingered in my cabin until I heard her climb the steps to hers. Kiara opened the door, and a scream punctuated the silence.

I stepped out onto my balcony. "Something on your mind?" I drew out the "s".

She was already on her balcony, glaring towards my cabin. Her face was red, and I could see she was holding back a smile. She grumbled under her breath and returned to her room before her angry face broke into laughter.

But, while I was celebrating my victory, she was scheming. And her last prank? It was a doozy.

We were taking photos in the garden as the guests went in for lunch.

"Wow golden boy, your photos are blown out. Haven't you tried adjusting the exposure?" She had my camera in her hands.

"Yes?"

She gave me a skeptical look and her brown eyes met mine. I couldn't keep a smile off my face. Kiara has a weird effect on me these days.

"Hey Jonathan, mind giving me a hand?" Randy called to me from across the garden. I turned to find her trying to lift a keg by herself.

I jogged over to the bar to give her a hand while Kiara adjusted the settings on my camera.

Randy, who it turns out is the outdoor bartender, needed

the help. She had not one but three kegs that she was trying
to lift and fit into their proper positions at the bar.

"Wow, Jonathan, you've got a knack for setting kegs up."
Randy gave me a high-five.

"Don't ask." I laughed before walking back over to Kiara.
She'd finished experimenting with my camera.

"Here." She handed the camera back to me. "And, check
it out, it's the perfect time to get photos of the flowers. Nath's
done such a magnificent job."

I took the camera and fit the neck strap over my head
before following her to a different area of the garden. Kiara
raised her camera and began taking photos.

I lifted my camera to take a few shots when I found
myself staring into the bulbous eyes of a small, slimy, purple
snail.

"Agh!"

I immediately dropped my camera, and it fell heavily
into the neck strap. Somehow, the snail survived the ride,
clinging onto the top of the camera for dear life.

Behind me, Kiara erupted in laughter.

I glared, carefully urged the snail onto my finger, and
placed it comfortably into the grass.

"You might want to be careful with your camera," Kiara
said, her eyes tearing from laughter. "They're pretty
expensive."

She thinks she's so funny. I grin, check my reflection in
the mirror one more time, and then pack up my toothbrush
and walk out from the bathroom block. I can't wait for the
next prank.

Kiara stands a little ways from the cabins, looking out
over the lake. She's wearing shorts and a hoodie, and her
hair is in a high ponytail.

She looks good with her hair up. I noticed it immediately when I saw her at the first garden party earlier this week. Her shorts and hoodies look great too, but I couldn't believe how hot she was in the black dress. She just seemed... effortlessly confident. I've never seen that side of her before.

I rush into my cabin and grab my camera. The sky is already starting to lighten and I need to get my head in the game.

"The Queen's up early this morning," I call out as I approach her.

She sighs dramatically. "It's the price I must pay for being a royal, I'm afraid."

I'm about to spend another day with Kiara, and as much as I'm loath to admit it — I don't hate the idea.

25
___

KIARA

*H*ow is the water so still?

The calm surface of the lake reflects the mountain peaks perfectly. In fact, everything around me feels quiet and unmoving this morning. I freeze, barely breathing, pretending that I'm one with this still image.

It's 5:30 in the morning and I've resolved to climb the mountain beside the Inn.

Jonathan and I were packing up last night when the idea came to me. We were down at the gazebo, and the last guest had disappeared for the night. It was just he and I, under the fairy lights I'd so carefully strung up days before.

"Well, Garcia, I've got to hand it to you, you've got the fairy lights down," Jonathan said, staring up at the doily shape.

"They almost *came* down when I was trying to put them up."

I immediately regretted my words. We hadn't talked about our first encounter at the Inn. I was holding my breath, wondering if Jonathan would clap back with a snarky comment.

"You're lucky I was here to save the day!" His denim eyes danced.

"Lucky, was it?" I laughed as I put my camera away.

He chuckled as he took a stand at the end of the gazebo, looking out over the lake. "So, what's your top bucket list item while you're here this summer?"

I paused. What should I tell him? Jonathan and I were on slightly friendlier terms this week. I was getting to know this new Jonathan, and to my surprise, he was actually funny. And almost cool.

But I wasn't sure I was ready to trust him yet. I didn't want to divulge the full truth behind my being here — I was still sore from Lucas' words all those years ago.

"Kicking your butt," I said, deciding to hedge. I went to stand at the opposite end of the gazebo floor. "Shouldn't be hard."

Behind him, the moon was shining brightly over the lake. The lights in the gazebo threw a warm glow on his face while he laughed, so he looked even more carefree than usual. With his blonde hair, chiseled features and lovely smile, it would've been a really nice photo. I fingered my camera bag, wondering if I should take it out.

"No, honestly." His eyes caught the moonlight and sparkled. "If you tell me yours, I'll tell you mine."

Was he serious? I chuckled, stalling for time. "I want to climb the mountain next to the Inn. Preferably for sunrise."

The words tumbled from my mouth without considera-tion. I hadn't thought about the mountain in days, but now that the words were out of my mouth, I realized how true they were.

"Then let's do it," he said, his voice low. "Tomorrow. 5:30am. Let's do it."

Another challenge. I can't say no to a challenge put forth by Jonathan Wright.

I smirked and narrowed my eyes. Was he teasing me? I'd never done something so spontaneous before. Usually, I planned something like this to prevent disasters.

But Jonathan was looking at me expectantly, and his smile made me feel surprisingly calm about the whole thing.

"Deal," I said as a smile broke out over my face. "Now, your turn."

"Okay, so, my top bucket list item—"

He walked towards me, and his eyes bore into mine. My heart sped up.

Get a grip, Kiara.

He stood in front of me, and I straightened instinctively. My legs felt numb, and I leaned back on the railing of the gazebo. He smelled nice, like shampoo and pine trees. He reached an arm beside me as though going in for a hug, and I realized I wasn't breathing.

"If you want to know, you'll have to catch me first." He flicked off the light switch for the gazebo, conveniently right next to me.

Laughing, he darted away.

I stood still, my heart racing. What just happened?

I chased after him, but he was already at his cabin.

"Bright and early, Garcia." He saluted me, ducked into his cabin, and locked the door.

I rolled my eyes, out of breath, as I made my way into my cabin.

I tried to convince myself the run had made me breathless, but I wasn't entirely sure that was the truth.

~

The sky slowly lightens towards dawn. I stand alone and look over the lake, feeling nervous.

Are we actually doing this? Are we going to try to scale a mountain in the dark? I don't like hiking at the best of times, but now it feels even less likely. What types of animals mill about when the daylight hits? Coyotes? Bears? Mountain lions? What if we run into one of them?

And what if Jonathan doesn't show up?

What if this is all just a big prank? Maybe he's watching from the bushes right now, snickering at the girl who thought they might actually be friends.

Should I go back to the cabin and forget this ever happened?

I don't want to bail, but I don't want to look like a fool, either. Or be eaten by a bear.

This is stupid.

I should just go back home.

"The Queen's up early this morning." Jonathan's voice brings the relief of lotion on a sunburn.

I fake a dramatic sigh. "It's the price I must pay for being a royal, I'm afraid."

Jonathan jogs over.

"Golden boy." I put my hands on my hips and feign impatience. "Late again."

He punches me playfully in the arm as we set off. But instead of going towards the lake, he heads towards the forest.

"Think you can keep up?" he asks, smiling over his shoulder. "I found a shortcut, but it might be too tough for your Majesty's delicate feet."

"You could always carry me. Like a good peasant." I grin.

He still calls me Queen and makes jokes about my royal lineage, but now that I've gotten to know him better, they don't feel mean. They're actually kind of fun, it's a little game we play. I'm relieved he's here — it means I don't have to climb the mountain alone.

We jog across the grounds towards the forest and I finally see what he's referring to. There is a break in the trees with a dirt path leading upward.

"Legacy Viewpoint," I say, reading the sign next to the trail. "Fantastic!"

Jonathan lets me go first, stopping whenever I need a break to catch my breath. Ava was right. Nature is *not* my thing, and gaining elevation is the bane of my existence. The things I do for photos.

Meanwhile, Jonathan practically jogs in circles around me.

"You're annoying," I say at one point, too exhausted and out of breath to come up with anything witty.

"So, is it time for me to carry you now?" Laughter twinkles in his eyes.

I glare and try to hold back a smile. Classic golden boy, being the best at everything.

Jonathan leads me through the last section of trail. The birds have started their maniacal morning song and butterflies flutter about. The sky lightens, and soon, the sun will peek over the mountains. Despite the burning in my legs, I walk with renewed purpose.

After what feels like the hundredth switchback, we reach a flattened piece of earth with a wooden platform.

I fall dramatically to the ground and take a deep breath. "We made it."

Jonathan laughs. "You know we have to go back down, right?"

"I'll roll."

I catch my breath, then sit up to enjoy the view.

It's perfect.

The sun hasn't peeked over the mountains and the sky is still a muted shade of dark blue. I whip out my camera, snap photos, check the results, and adjust for the eventual sunrise.

"This view is amazing," I say.

Jonathan, however, isn't looking at the view. He's turned towards the mountain, looking up. I follow his gaze and see what he's looking at. We aren't far from the summit of the Legacy Mountain and there's a rough trail for hikers far more daring than me.

On one hand, any photos taken at the summit will be better than photos taken here. On the other, it means more hiking. And it's not the clear dirt path we followed to get to the viewpoint. The trail is rough and overgrown with thorny shrubs.

"Are you thinking..."

"Scared?" He turns towards me with a challenge in his eyes.

How could I back down?

Jonathan leads the way up the rough trail, holding back branches and brambles as we go so I don't get scratched. It's a suspiciously kind move and I narrow my eyes every time he does it, expecting him to let go of a branch so it smacks me in the face. He never does, though.

We reach the summit and look out over the panorama. It's breathtakingly beautiful.

From up here, we can see the Inn and the garden, along with the surrounding forest. Behind us, the mountains of the National Park are dark, unmoving masses. The lake reflects the white-capped peaks ahead of us, and a ripple makes them disappear into oblivion. The sun is just starting to rise, and the sky is now shades of pastel. The air is brisk and fresh, smelling of morning dew. It's colder up here, but that's not the reason I have goosebumps.

This view. This absolutely perfect view.

I whip the camera to my face and urgently take photos. I've never seen anything like it.

Snap. Snap. Snap. I watch the sunrise from the screen of my camera. It's unbelievable. I hope the photos do it justice.

Jonathan, however, is silent. He took a couple of photos, but he's now standing still, eyes on the horizon. His camera hangs from his neck.

"Don't you want to get this?" I ask, my brow furrowed. "How many times will we see something like this?"

He keeps his eyes on the horizon as the sky becomes vibrant shades of pink and red.

"Exactly," he says. "Why not just enjoy the moment?"

I frown, considering his words, and peek over my camera at the vista before me. For the first time since the sun started to rise, I lower my camera. I let go, letting it hang from the neck strap, just as he's doing.

My breath catches as I watch the sky change from moment to moment. I rarely let myself enjoy a beautiful view for what it is. I usually need to capture the scene as best as I can while the wonderful, inspiring, shocking action is happening.

Is this what it means to live in the moment? My heart is racing.

26

JONATHAN

The sky is changing by the second and I don't want to blink.

Slowly, I sit, carefully holding my camera. Kiara is as blown away as I am. She takes a seat next to me and we watch the sun rise in a comfortable silence.

"It's the golden hour," she says, her voice low and happy.

Golden hour? I'm about to ask when she reads my mind.

"It's the time right after sunrise. See? The light is softer and warmer, and the shadows don't seem as harsh. It's just calm, happy, peaceful."

I tear my eyes from the horizon to look at her. I'm captivated. She's beautiful. Her dark hair frames her face and her eyes are filled with wonder. She takes one last photo and then lets the camera hang in front of her. I don't want to look away, but I know that I'm staring.

The golden hour washes over us. For all of my early morning workouts, I've never taken the time to appreciate the sunrise. I did a lot of my morning training sessions inside, or if we were outside, I was usually too distracted by my coach to pay attention to my surroundings.

"One of my first memories is of the sunrise," I say without thinking. "I was with my parents."

Kiara is so close her knee is touching mine. The words come easily, without thought. It's an unfamiliar feeling, seeing as I usually have to monitor my every breath.

"We were traveling together when I was a kid. We used to do these insane road trips over to California or Texas or Florida — we'd just get in the car and drive."

I smile and my breath catches. "I remember one morning, back when I was 4, my dad got us up early. He wanted to beat the crowds to one of the beaches in California. I was sleeping in the back seat, but I opened my eyes right as the sun was rising. The sky was so colorful, I'd never seen anything like it. My parents were holding hands in the front. It felt like the world stopped. It was the happiest I've ever been."

I remember it all. The colors in the sky, the flat road ahead of us, the quiet in the car. It's a still image in my mind, the place I return to anytime I'm stressed or unhappy. I've been visiting the memory more and more over recent years.

And then, my smile fades. "The next year, my parents started putting me into every soccer camp in Edendale. I joined league after league to eventually become the 'star midfielder' of the Eagles." My fingers form quotation marks around the words. "That sunrise feels like the last thing I really enjoyed before they started expecting so much. Before they wanted me to become a big-time soccer player with a full-ride scholarship."

Back then, my parents were happy and carefree. Now, they frown when I come into the room. Soccer weighs on them as much as it weighs on me. It's the prison we're all trapped inside.

To my surprise, Kiara's soft hand reaches for mine, giving it a squeeze.

"What about photography?" she asks.

I laugh bitterly as a much less pleasant memory comes back to me. "They would be horrified to hear that I want to pursue photography. They never wanted this for me. In fact—"

How much can I say? How much should I tell her? I glance over and Kiara's looking at me with a question in her eyes. Her gaze is soft and kind.

"It was a photo you took that got me into trouble."

Her brow furrows and a fire lights in her eyes.

Did I say too much? I instantly regret not phrasing my words better. But, in a matter of seconds, her face relaxes and her mouth pops open.

"Oh. *That* photo?" she asks.

I nod silently, thinking back to the image that plastered the front of our school's newspaper last fall — the photo that had created waves with so many of my friends and family. It's a beautiful photo, there's no doubt. It's well-shot and I could hardly believe the person in the picture was me.

"It didn't take long for Coach to recognize me." My voice is quiet, like the golden hour has hushed everything in its glow. "Then my teammates and friends, and finally my parents. I almost got kicked off of the Eagles because of it. It took a very long time to convince Coach to let me stay on the team and to make it up to my teammates. My parents *still* bring it up with me whenever we get into arguments."

I shrug, remembering the months of work it took to make reparations. It's part of the reason I shoved my camera into the back of my closet for so long. Now, I wouldn't dare even say the words "photo" or "camera" around my closest friends and family.

"I'm sorry, Jonathan." Kiara says, her voice sincere. "I didn't know."

Her words feel like a balm, and I realize how much of my dislike for her has been grounded in that one action from last fall. The very thing that separated us was a grudge I held without thought. I never considered that she might not *know* how much that photo had affected my life. Given that she would still make the occasional sassy remark to that point, I assumed she knew exactly what she was doing when she published the photo.

"It's okay," I finally say, realizing that it's true. A heavy weight is lifting off of me. "Honestly, it was about time my parents figured out how much I like photography."

Kiara has that cute half-smile again, but her eyes are sympathetic. The glow of the sunlight on her face makes her look ethereal. Her eyes meet mine and it's like the golden hour is shining from within her.

Her photo got me in so much trouble, but why do I feel grateful for it now?

J've stopped breathing. For once, I don't force myself to look away from Jonathan's eyes, and I let the moment engulf us. The sun feels warm on my cheeks already, and the stillness in the air feels like magic.

Emotions roar through me. The photo that Jonathan is referring to is the same one that got me this year's award with our newspaper.

I took the photo last fall, during one of the first Eagles games of the season. I arrived late, as usual, and by the time I got to the field, the Eagles were 20 minutes into the first half. I stood off to the side, tucked in by the bleachers.

As I made my way along the bleachers, however, I came across an unusual sight. A guy with a dark jacket and a beanie was standing just ahead of me with his own camera.

From the back, I remember thinking the guy seemed attractive. He was leaning casually against the side of the bleachers, effortlessly confident, and he appeared artsy. He snapped a photo of the game as the Eagles were celebrating a goal.

It was such an unusual moment that I took my own

photo. The guy's profile was clear — he had a chiseled jawline and blonde hair peeking out of the side of the beanie. It was a stark contrast to the dark outfit and the darker bleachers.

The flash from my camera caught the guy's attention, and he whirled around. The "artsy guy" was none other than Jonathan Wright — the Eagles' star soccer player who should have been playing.

My jaw dropped.

His shock turned to rage, and he glared at me before running off.

I stood still, barely able to register what had just happened. Why was Jonathan Wright taking photos of the game instead of playing it? I brushed off the question as "weird golden boy behavior" and continued taking photos for the newspaper.

A few days later, I was going through all the game photos with the editor and we came across the image.

"Kiara, this photo is *exceptional*," Abby said as she pulled up the image on her screen and enlarged it. I'm proud of most of my work, but I'll admit that this photo was particularly good. The scene was moody, dark and *real*, contrasting perfectly with the celebrations on the field. "We need to publish this."

I frowned at her words. Given his rage when he saw me, I had the feeling that Jonathan was not supposed to be there on that day.

"I don't know, Abby," I said, trying to take the spotlight off the photo. "It's not really a proper photo of the game."

"So? Who cares?" Abby flailed her hands around.

Was she joking? Abby may have been new to the editorial team, but she *must've* known this. "Literally the entire population of Edendale."

Abby sighed. "Yeah, I guess so. Still, this shot is a one-in-a-million for our paper."

I blushed, then scrambled for another excuse. "I just don't think it'll do well with the student population. They want to see the action, not some random guy taking photos of the action."

As I said the words, I knew they were true. The students at our school wouldn't be interested in a well-shot image of a guy taking photos at a soccer game. If they knew that the guy was Jonathan, that might change...

Despite my lingering anger with him for his false "nice guy" persona, I couldn't fathom throwing him under the bus. I could always publish the image with another magazine or newspaper once we'd graduated.

"No way," Abby insisted as she played with cropping the photo onto the front page. "This needs to be in the next issue."

"I'm not sure..."

Abby swiveled around on her chair to face me, her eyes wide and questioning over the tops of her round glasses. "Kiara, you want to be a photographer, yeah? You'll want this photo in your portfolio, trust me. It's fantastic. Don't sell yourself short."

I frowned again, looking at the photo over her shoulder. It was hard to tell that it was Jonathan. The jawline and blonde hair were the only indications. The only reason I knew it was him was because he turned around and scowled at me.

"Do you recognize the student, by any chance?" I said vaguely.

Abby swiveled back around and leaned in towards the screen.

"No." She pushed her glasses up. "Does he go here?"

That was all the verification I needed. I smiled and gave Abby the go ahead. If she couldn't recognize the profile of Jonathan Wright, surely no one else would?

I was wrong.

The gossip flew once it got out that Jonathan had purposely skipped an important game to take photos. There were rumors that the coach would kick him off the team. There were rumors that his friend group had ousted him and that he had lost his chance for scholarships.

But whenever I saw Jonathan, he was smiling and happy. He seemed unfazed by the rumors and gossip, which led me to believe that none of them were true. When his snarky comments and insults started ramping up, I figured it was because he hated the photo. It appears I was wrong about that too.

And now, sitting here in a loaded silence, the golden hour upon us, I see his side of things. It's unbelievable that one seemingly meaningless moment can change someone's future.

"I'm not sorry for the photo," I whisper, not wanting to break the spell between us. "But I am sorry for how it affected your life."

He tilts his head, and I wonder if he'll be upset. Unexpectedly, his face breaks into a smile and my heart skips a beat.

"I'm not sorry for the photo either. Besides, you really captured my good side," he says jokingly, a twinkle in his eye.

Then his voice turns serious. "You know that you're the only one who knows this about me? Knows why I'm here?"

I want to reach for his hand again. "And so what? If I tell your secret, you'll have to kill me?"

He raises his eyebrows. "Why do you think I brought you to the top of a mountain?"

I laugh. "Well, I know one way to protect myself."

"What's that?"

"Photo evidence." I lean my head in so it's almost on his shoulder and point my camera at us. "Say Legacy!"

Click.

I check the picture. We look almost natural together.

Get a grip! I push that thought out of my head.

"Let me see." Jonathan takes the camera from my hands and grins. "Even when you're not looking through the lens you're better than I am."

I laugh and bump my shoulder against his.

He chuckles. "It's funny, I've been training for soccer tirelessly over the last few years—"

"No. Shocking."

He makes a face and then turns serious. "Somehow, despite all that training, I'm not sure I'll ever be good enough for everyone around me."

Silence falls over us as I consider Jonathan's words. Edendale's golden boy — the star midfielder for the Eagles — doubts his abilities?

"No... you do well, soccer." I say awkwardly, tripping over my words. *Phenomenal job, Kiara.*

Jonathan glances at me and bursts out laughing.

"What I mean is," I say, smiling, "I know *nothing* about soccer, but it *seems* like you know what you're doing."

He chuckles as our eyes meet. "It's nothing compared to your photos. You've got a genuine talent, Kiara. I'm honestly so impressed by what you can do. But if you tell anyone I said that, I'll deny, deny, deny."

Unmistakable butterflies fill my stomach. It feels like the entire world has turned upside down.

A week ago, I believed that Jonathan Wright and I were opposites, destined to be rivals, my grandchildren would despise his grandchildren. But a week into my time at Legacy Inn, the only thing I was right about is that Jonathan *does* put up a front. Though it's entirely different from the one I expected.

"I hope you're right," I say, my voice sad.

I hug my knees to my chest and relive what happened last week, right before I came to the Inn.

Am I doing this? For some inexplicable reason, I want to tell him. His words struck a chord with me — I know exactly how he feels. Our little spot on this summit feels magical, like a room for secrets that will always be kept safe.

"I was... rejected by a magazine. The Glacier Journal," I say, staring flatly towards the bright horizon. The sun rises over the mountains. "They said that my photos weren't good enough. I believe their exact words were 'lifeless and dull'."

Frustrated tears sting my eyes and I squeeze my knees tighter to my chest. "Photography is all I've ever wanted to do. It's all I *can* do. And on my first try, I'm called lifeless and dull."

Shame burns bright at the sting of the memory. I've been hiding my disappointment, but it's lingering just below the surface.

"The Inn is my chance to capture 'lifelike' photos for Glacier," I say. "It's the only way I can build up a good enough portfolio to get out of Edendale after graduation."

I sigh before continuing. "You say your parents care too much about where you are this summer. I can't imagine what that's like. My mom couldn't care less. My dream has always been to leave for good and get out of her hair. I think it's her dream too. My photos? They're my best shot."

Just like I'd done for him, Jonathan reaches out and

grabs my hand. His hand is big and warm, and his touch feels electrifying.

The emotional storm inside ebbs as we gaze out towards the horizon, our hands clasped tight around the magic of our confessions.

28
─────

JONATHAN

iara's hand fits naturally in mine as we look towards the mountain peaks. We'll have to return to the Inn soon, but I don't want this moment to end.

I never would have imagined that Kiara the Queen acted the way she did for a good reason. The nickname sounds weak now.

"I didn't know," I say, regretting all the times me and my teammates used the name.

"Sure you did," Kiara snaps, but her voice is sad.

She takes her hand out of mine and places it back around her knees.

"Don't you remember?" She refuses to meet my eyes. Her face is a mask of angry determination.

I rack my brains, digging into the past. We've had our squabbles and arguments over the years. I must've said something that crossed the line. What was it?

I wave the white flag, admitting defeat. "I can't remember."

Kiara exhales loudly and I wait for what she has to say. We have all day up here, if she wants it.

"It was the first Eagles game." Her voice wavers. "My first job as a photographer with the school's newspaper."

She recounts the exact moment that I've tried hard to forget, to push deep into my memory. Never in my life have I acted so badly towards someone. Lucas' comment and the laughter from the team still rings in my ears, and to this day, I'm deeply ashamed about what I did.

Because of that moment, I attempt to stand up for anyone I notice is getting picked on. But it will never make up for what happened with Kiara when we were freshmen — the moment I was too chicken to stand up for her.

"Kiara." I struggle to find the right words. "I think about that moment almost every day."

She sits silent, still. She's taken her sunglasses from her camera bag and they hide her eyes.

"I can't tell you how sorry I am that I didn't stand up for you. You know Lucas, he always makes those stupid comments..." I trail off, realizing that I'm making an excuse.

"I had just got on the team, I was trying to fit in. I made a bad call, I'll be the first to admit it. Lucas has gotten worse over the years, and I barely talk to him anymore."

I roll my eyes thinking of my supposed "friend" and teammate. "I should have said something."

Kiara is still frozen and my heart hurts.

"You know I tried to apologize?" I say, my voice quiet.

"What? No you didn't."

"I did, plenty of times. Didn't you think it was weird that I kept asking to be on group projects with you and I waited for you after class? You kept avoiding me and making these snide comments, so eventually, I snapped back."

I look at my hands, seeing as she won't meet my eyes. "Then the photo got published, and I was in a mess of trouble. And now I'm here. Sitting on a mountain hoping that you'll forgive me. Or, at least not push me off."

Kiara is a stone statue and I'm staring down, hoping she understands. There are no words that could cover how ashamed I feel for my behavior.

After two minutes, she reaches for her camera. She lifts her sunglasses to look through the viewfinder, but I can see the pain behind her eyes. "I won't be pushing you off the mountain. At least not today." She sighs. "We both messed up."

"We did," I agree. "But now we're here, taking photos. And you get to kick my butt with your amazing shots."

"Amazingly DULL shots." She rolls her eyes, her cute half-smile coming back.

I laugh, feeling elated. I'd do anything to see her smile. And then, I know what we need to do.

"I have an idea," I say. "Come with me."

She looks at me, rather bemused, and I grab her hand and we both jog down the mountain. By the time we reach the cabins, I've got a plan.

"Where are we going? What's going on?" she asks. The other students are still waking up and getting ready, so we have a bit of time.

"Put on your bathing suit if you want to find out. And leave your camera."

"*Leave* my camera? It's like you don't know me."

I smile, grabbing her hand. "Just trust me."

"Why?" She frowns, clearly skeptical. There's a war in her eyes as she debates following me — the insane "golden boy" from high school.

I shrug, feigning nonchalance. "Well, for starters, I didn't push you off a mountain. Even though I so clearly could've."

A smile crosses her lips, and she gives me a playful punch, turning on her heel.

"You sure have a funny idea of what 'trust' is, golden boy." She retreats into her cabin.

Will she trust me? I stand for a moment, hoping that she comes back out.

After a few minutes, I shift from foot to foot nervously. There's silence from her cabin.

It's not looking good.

Then, her door pops open and she emerges wearing just her shorts and tank top over her bathing suit. Her camera is nowhere to be found.

"Great choice." I grab her hand and lead her towards the forest on the other side of the cabins.

Over the last week, when I wasn't trying to keep up with Kiara, or prank her, I'd spent some time exploring the grounds. There's a sweet little spot that I doubt she's come across, but it will change her perspective completely.

I just hope she likes it. I'm surprisingly nervous. When I was dating Isabella or the other girls at school, I never thought much about impressing them. But with Kiara, it's a different ballgame.

We reach the creek flowing peacefully through the forest. It eventually runs into the lake, but I turn in the opposite direction, heading towards thicker trees. I'm careful to hold branches back so they don't scratch her. She's suspiciously silent.

"Scared yet?" I joke, squeezing her hand.

"A little scared you might murder me."

"Don't worry, we're almost there."

The trees thin, and the creek widens. We climb along the edge of a small canyon, the blue water shining bright just below. The water is gentle, flowing lazily through the canyon.

There's a small perch not too far up from the water. I slow to a stop, and she stands close to me on the perch.

I put my arms around her before her questioning gaze meets mine.

I grin. "We're going to jump."

29

KIARA

*D*id Jonathan just say we're going to JUMP? No. That can't be right. Only a crazy person—

"Are you ready? Let's jump!"

So he *is* crazy.

"I'm sorry. WHAT?"

I'm trying not to be distracted by Jonathan's arms wrapped tight around me, soccer has done wonderful things for his body. But the minute he said "jump", my stomach flipped over and not in a good way.

"Let's do it!" His blue eyes dance.

"Are you insane? No way am I jumping from here," I say, daring to take a peek over the ledge.

"As a matter of fact, I am insane. But so are you. In your own way."

Every instinct wants me to run screaming from the ledge. "It's like a 20-foot drop!"

Jonathan steps away, and I almost fall over. I'm feeling very vulnerable on the perch all alone.

"Get back here!" I command, grasping his arm and pulling him close to me for protection.

"What did I say back there?" He gazes into my eyes.

"Uh. That you're a crazy person who has a death wish?"

He laughs. "I never said that."

"You didn't have to."

He rolls his eyes.

"Just trust me." The end of the sentence almost forms a question. "I'm jumping with you."

He slides his hand down my arm and then holds his hand out for me to take it. He turns towards the water.

There's no reason for me to trust him. He's just the golden boy, the star soccer player who gets his entire life handed to him. His kind and charming facade might truly be an act, and all of his confessions this morning could be false.

I'm aware of these things, these "facts" that seemed undeniable until this past week. But everything I thought I knew about Jonathan feels off. I believed his words this morning, I believed him because, for the first time, I think he was being sincere.

Is there more to Jonathan Wright than just the Edendale golden boy? I contemplate the question as he waits patiently for my decision. Somehow, for no sensible reason, everything in my gut tells me I can believe him about this too. I can trust him.

Wordlessly, I place my hand in his.

Facing the water, I take a deep breath. It feels absurdly high up.

"On three?" he asks.

"On three." I swallow my nerves.

"One."

We're so high up, I'm light-headed.

"Two."

And how cold is the water? What if there's something in it, just waiting to devour me whole? I can't do this.

"Three."

I squeeze my eyes shut and my scream can be heard from miles away as I leap into space.

30

KIARA

*S*econds later, a cold shock envelops me as we hit the water. My muscles freeze and I let go of Jonathan's hand. I open my eyes and see the blue light of day shining at the surface.

All at once, my fears and inhibitions drop away. I have one goal — to reach the surface.

My muscles unclench as the mass of white bubbles around me fades. I kick my feet and flail my arms awkwardly, trying to remember my childhood swim classes. Every movement brings a shock of icy water swirling around me. I've never felt so awake, so alive.

My feet are working. I'm pleased to find that they aren't contacting anything but fresh mountain water. There's nothing beneath us, no nasty algae, no strange creek creature.

Slowly, I propel myself towards the surface, swimming through a beam of sunlight. My heart races as my arms slice through the freezing water.

I stop and float just beneath the surface, amazed that the sun's rays can warm my face, even underwater.

Finally, as my lungs burn, I break through the surface towards the sun, letting out a loud laugh.

"That was amazing!" I exclaim, laughing and splashing as Jonathan rises to the surface.

But something's wrong. His arms are a windmill of white and his mouth is full of water. "Help, I can't swim!"

Jonathan's flailing, his arms are wild and his voice is panicked.

Terror grips me.

I dog-paddle to him as fast as I can.

"I've got you!" I shout, battling through the mass of white water around him.

What do I do? How can I help him? Panic spreads through me.

I reach for him and I almost touch him.

He stops struggling.

He ducks below the surface and swims between my arms, emerging behind me.

Then he grasps my shoulders and dunks me under the surface.

When I come back up, sputtering, he's laughing his head off.

"That is not how you're supposed to treat your queen!" I shriek, swimming over to him and trying to get on his shoulders.

He shrugs me off, and I topple into the water, laughing hard. He grabs me around my midsection and tries to shimmy behind me to get out of the way of my arms. I whip around and try to get on his shoulders again.

Within moments, we're wrestling. He's circling his arms around my body, trying to dodge my attempts at punching his chest and dunking him. He swims just out of my grasp.

At one point, I finally grab the back of his neck, ready to

plunge his face underwater, when he wraps me in a bear hug and I lose all downward momentum.

"No fair." I laugh as he squeezes me tight to his chest. "You have a height advantage."

Jonathan's eyes are glittering, and he's smiling. "As far as I can tell, the only advantage I have is that I have you in my arms."

His face freezes, and I blush at his words. What? Is he saying he *wants* me in his arms? I don't think that's what he meant.

He breaks into bashful laughter and I laugh along with him, feeling his chest move beneath my fingers.

My body feels warm, electric. The world is brighter. Never in my life have I felt so alive, so exhilarated. Adrenaline pumps through my body and my face hurts from smiling.

Then our laughter dies as his eyes meet mine. There's an intensity between us. One I haven't noticed before.

Is he going to kiss me?

My heart speeds up as I realize that I want nothing more than this very moment, his lips on mine.

He places his hand tenderly at the back of my head and I lean in. The warmth of his body is intoxicating.

My teeth chatter together loudly, a repetitive clack clack clack that completely kills the moment.

Am I cold? I didn't realize.

Jonathan examines my arms, which are covered in goosebumps. "You're freezing."

"I'm fine," I say through my chattering teeth.

"Let's swim to shore. It's time we get back to the Inn, anyway." Jonathan smiles and lets me go.

Ugh. Way to ruin the moment, Kiara. I'm cursing myself as we swim, wishing we could go back to just seconds before.

Jonathan wraps a big towel around me and rubs my arms up and down, warming me up. I smile as I take in his lovely face creased in concentration.

This morning is the most alive I've felt since... forever.

Then, a crazy thought comes to me. Could Jonathan help give my photos some life?

31

KIARA

I clutch my camera to my chest and run down the path towards the Inn. My white Converse kick up dirt, and I'm hoping they won't look too scuffy by the time I get to the garden. I'm wearing a butter yellow mini-dress that Ava forced me to buy ages ago. It's the first time I've worn it, and I have to admit, she has an eye for color.

I smooth my dress as I approach the bustling chatter in the garden. I glance over my shoulder at the lake — the sun is going down and we're just about at the evening golden hour. It's the perfect time to capture photos of the guests.

I walk into the garden party, a giant smile on my face. I'll admit — I'm excited to see Jonathan.

It's been a few days since we jumped into the river, he held me in his arms, and we shared our secrets on the mountain. Since then, every day with him has been exhilarating. My face hurts from the constant smiling and laughter. Wild butterflies break loose when he catches my eye.

And when I think about our almost-kiss? My lips tingle and I blush. It was almost a kiss, wasn't it? Will he ever kiss me?

Silly, Kiara. Don't go there. Past Kiara, the Kiara from last week — the one who never jumped feet first into a mountain creek, the one who hid her rejection from Glacier Journal, the one who hated Jonathan Wright — would never think or hope for such things.

Yet, as I head to the dance floor and gaze over the guests, I'm practically giddy with excitement.

"You okay, Ki?"

Nath's voice breaks me from my reverie. I stop biting my lower lip and gazing dreamily into space, standing up straight instead.

"Why do you ask?"

Nath gives me a skeptical look. She can see right through me. "No reason. You're just looking a little... flushed."

I cough to hide another blush and turn away to look over the crowd once again. I can't see Jonathan anywhere, and my heart falls slightly.

Where is he? I thought he wanted to hang around with the guests tonight? The crowd is a mass of colorful blues, pinks, yellows and greens. But there is a distinct lack of the one person I long to see — though I'd never tell *him* that.

With a sigh, I turn on my camera and get ready to take photos of the guests.

This afternoon, Jonathan and I were hanging out in the hammocks, swinging lazily. Jonathan convinced me to skip the Legacy summit so we could stay up late with the guests this evening.

"I think I'm gonna go to my cabin," I said with a yawn. "It's too bright out here to nap."

Jonathan chuckled, and his chest rumbled beneath my cheek. "We can do something else if you want."

What did he mean by *that*? I sat up straight in the

hammock and glared down at him. His blue eyes widened for a second as he realized how that sounded.

"No, no." He laughed. "I meant we can, like, play soccer or pool or something."

I hopped out of the hammock and slipped my flip-flops back on my feet.

"You don't want to play pool with me. I just don't think you'll be able to handle losing again."

Jonathan burst into laughter and then circled his arms around me, bringing me close. His face was almost level with mine as I was leaning over.

"Is that what you think?"

His arms were strong around my waist. I glanced down at his lips. Ugh, I wanted to kiss him so bad.

And then he leaned away, swinging back into the hammock. "You may be winning the social media posts. But I have a few tricks up my sleeve, Garcia."

"We'll see about that, golden boy."

With that, I jogged back to my cabin. My heart was racing and I couldn't keep a blush off my face. It's no wonder all I can think about is kissing Jonathan Wright.

When I woke up after my nap, the feeling was much less pleasant. I was already late for the garden party *and* I couldn't find my camera. In a panic, I dove to the ground to check under my bed. I checked the dresser, the nightstand, my suitcase, everywhere. My camera was nowhere to be found.

Heart racing and feeling nauseous, I threw on my dress, brushed out my hair and ran outside. I looked on my balcony, in the bathroom block, at the student picnic table, but it wasn't there.

My panic was rising quickly, and my vision was hazy.

The hammocks! I ran full-tilt towards the hammocks.

When I arrived, my heart exploded with relief. There it was. Sitting on a small table by the hammocks, exactly where I left it, untouched. Jonathan had vacated the area, and I figured he must not have seen it before he left.

"You're fine!" I whispered to my camera, cradling it like a newborn.

Now, as I click on my camera — my beloved camera — I'm shocked for a moment that such a thing could have happened. That's another thing Past Kiara would never have done. Leaving her camera behind, and with her nemesis? Blasphemy.

The screen powers up, and a photo appears.

The photo on the screen shows a piece of paper with my name.

Kiara

Heart racing, I click through. There's another photo after this one.

meet

Another word on a piece of paper.

me

My heart races as I click through the rest of the photos. My breath is shallow, my face hot. Butterflies are no longer contained to my stomach, it's as if they're swirling around me, a nervous tornado.

I click through the photos again to make sure they say what I think they say.

They do.

Kiara, meet me at the gazebo at midnight. Yours, Golden Boy.

32

JONATHAN

*T*he full moon shines bright into the gazebo as I wait for Kiara to arrive. It's midnight and I'm smiling even as my insides are twisting with nerves.

It's been a few days since we cliff jumped and shared our secrets on the mountain. A few days since I had her in my arms. A few days since we almost kissed. It's a moment I can't get out of my head.

I should have kissed her. What if I don't get another chance?

My feelings for Kiara have grown stronger every day. Every minute with her feels effortless and wonderful. We've fallen into a comfortable rhythm — in a way similar to our banter at school, but the emotions behind our conversations are so different. It's crazy to think that my perceptions about her were dead wrong. At Edendale High, we were all about nagging each other. But now, she's the only person I feel truly myself with.

We've also developed a routine, just the two of us. We wake up early most mornings to catch the sunrise on the Legacy summit. Somehow, it feels brighter and more beautiful each day. In the afternoons, we nap in the hammocks close to the cabins while the guests have lunch.

Today we took a day off from our routine. We skipped out on the sunrise this morning in order to stay up later with the guests. Or, that's how I justified it to Kiara when I suggested it.

"Come on, golden boy, you just didn't want another early morning!" She laughed as we swung together on a hammock this afternoon.

"Guilty as charged," I said, holding back my smile.

Yesterday, I decided it was time to ask her on a date. I have a whole evening planned out, and I got a lot of inspiration from stories my dad used to tell me about when he met my mom.

To drum up the suspense, I showed up to the garden party early, took a few photos, and left before she arrived. For the first time this summer, we didn't spend the evening working together.

Now, it's past midnight and I'm hoping that my plan worked.

And that she *wants* to show up. I remember her words from one of our first days here. She joked that she only dates photographers or, at the very least, "artsy types". Whatever that means. She never said she would date a soccer player.

The minutes tick on and the world around me is silent. A small voice nags at me. Is she coming?

I check my watch. 12:10.

What if she still sees me as "golden boy Jonathan" from Edendale High? I wouldn't blame her. I could've been kinder to her in the past. I regret those times now, but an apology only goes so far. She might've seen the note and thought it wasn't worth it. I can understand why she was angry with me for so long, and why she wouldn't want to date me now.

I fiddle with my hands, looking out towards the lake and listening for any sound coming down the path.

12:15.

With every minute counting down on my watch, my heart sinks further, and the voice gets louder. Did I read her all wrong? All I've been able to think about lately is kissing her, showing her how much she means to me. Is it entirely one-sided?

I sigh and my shoulders slump as I stare at the ground. What do I do? How long should I wait?

12:20.

The world is still around me. Even the surface of the lake doesn't have a single ripple. There are no birds or bugs making noise. It's just me and a deafening silence.

Then I hear a crunch in the distance.

Footsteps down the gravel path. Is that her?

I shift from foot to foot, the nerves taking over. Please let that be her.

12:25.

The footsteps are getting closer, and my heartbeat is rising. What if it's Delia or Vin? I'm definitely not meant to be out here right now. They'll be mad. Will they send me home?

The gravel path crunches loudly as the person turns the corner. I'm holding my breath, praying that it isn't Delia or Vin.

My stomach drops. I'd recognize that hair anywhere.

It's Kiara, wearing her jean shorts and a lacy top. Her hair is tumbling down her shoulders in waves. She catches my eye and smiles shyly, the moon illuminating her features beautifully.

Relief floods my senses, and I could almost kiss her right there and then. "You look amazing."

"Sorry, I'm late," she says at the same time.

I take her hands in mine and her half-smile breaks out over her face.

"I truly am," she whispers, blushing.

Right now, I could believe that we're the only two people in the world.

Feeling giddy and light-headed with happiness, I take her hand and lead her down the gravel path towards the lake.

Here we go.

33

KIARA

*J*onathan's hand is warm in mine as he leads me along the moonlit path. My heart is beating so loud, I wonder if he can hear it.

Despite my distraction tonight, I got some great photos of the guests. I've taken a page from Jonathan's book and have started speaking with the guests and engaging them. I'm not scrambling to get the shot anymore; the photos come naturally now.

I smiled like an idiot throughout the evening as I thought about him. Jonathan has this incredible way of relaxing me and making me feel at ease. When I'm around him, I *want* to be carefree. He brings out a side of me that feels alive.

Finally, when the last guest went to bed, I ran to my cabin to get ready. I debated keeping my dress on or wearing a skirt, but I always feel best when wearing my shorts. I let my hair down so it's falling in nice waves and then reapplied a bit of mascara.

The end result feels good to me — natural and confident.

Now, as Jonathan leads me along the lakeshore, I'm grateful for my choice. He's wearing his cute hoodie and board shorts. He must prefer this style to the designer shirts and fancy slacks he wears at Edendale High. We round the corner and I open my mouth to compliment him when a beautiful scene unfolds before me.

A secluded part of the beach lies ahead of us and the stars above are unobstructed. Jonathan has placed a bunch of fake candles in a circle. In the middle, a picnic basket and a blanket are laid out on the sand.

He sits on the far end of the blanket and shyly motions for me to come and sit next to him.

"Do you like it?"

I realize my mouth is still open and I clamp it shut. Speechless, I sit down next to him, gazing out over the lake. The calm surface mirrors the billions of stars above.

"Kiara?"

"It's incredible."

I take in the tapestry of stars above us. It feels like every constellation in the universe is visible.

Jonathan opens the picnic basket and takes out a container of food and some orange juice. My stomach grumbles.

He opens the lid of the container. "Mac and cheese."

"Fantastic choice. Jonathan." His name rolls off my tongue.

"Woah, Garcia, this is huge! I don't think you've ever called me by my name before!"

I roll my eyes dramatically. "There's a first time for everything."

We dig into the mac and cheese, eating by the light of the candles and the moon. We talk about everything and nothing. The more I get to know Jonathan, the more I realize that he's never what I expect. He has interesting perspectives on things I've always taken for granted.

In return, I get the gratifying feeling that he listens to what I have to say. He pays attention and asks intelligent questions. Our conversations flow easily, and sometimes I believe we could talk forever.

After we finish the mac and cheese, Jonathan turns to face me with a twinkle in his eyes. "We have one more thing to do."

He stands up and grabs two candles. He then runs down to the water's edge.

"You're insane!" I exclaim, and then laugh as he motions for me to follow.

But I guess I'm insane too. I grab two more candles and follow him down to the water. Together, we line the four candles by the water's edge.

"Now what?" I whisper excitedly.

Jonathan looks at me, a smile on his face. "We light the water."

He carefully grabs one candle and places it in the lake, pushing it out and away from us. I watch, mesmerized, as the flicking light floats away from the shoreline, creating ripples that disturb the perfect reflection.

As the light comes to a stop, the reflection on the water is unreal. It looks like a star, shining bright from beyond, or below, our atmosphere. The ripples fade, and I'm breathless.

"Can I try?" I ask, still spellbound by the beautiful sight.

"Absolutely."

Jonathan sits behind me, his legs around mine. We send the other three fake candles into the water together and I watch as the scene changes. We'll pick up the candles tomorrow, but for now, I allow myself to get lost in the view.

My hands instinctively reach for a camera that isn't there. I'd left it in my cabin.

A smile spreads across my face and I lean back onto his chest, appreciating the moment for all that it is. I rise and fall with his breath, his body warm against mine.

"So, Jonathan." A happy feeling overcomes me as I say his name. "I think you owe me something."

"What's that?"

"You owe me *your* top bucket list item."

He chuckles easily. The sound floats across the surface of the water. "You're right. I never told you that."

He pulls me closer, wrapping his arms around me. I lean into him, feeling at home.

"My top bucket list item," he whispers into my ear, "was to watch a sunrise with Kiara Garcia on a mountaintop."

I laugh and a blush spreads over my face. We sit in silence for a moment, feeling content. The stars reflect perfectly in the water, the moonlight illuminating the peaks in the distance. Everything about this moment is perfect.

"I have a new bucket list item..." I say, feeling brave.

"Yeah?"

Jonathan's voice is low and encouraging. I take a deep breath and I'm sure he can feel my heart racing. I'm not one to shy away from what I want, but I've never been this forward before.

"To kiss Jonathan Wright." My voice is more confident than I feel.

He's gone silent, stock still.

Did I go too far?

Then, he shifts me gently to the side so I can look up at him. The moon, the candles, and the stars reflect in his eyes. It's like they're holding the key to the future.

I tilt my chin.

He leans in.

Then, in the silence of the mountains, his lips meet mine, and the world stops.

It's just me, Jonathan, and the stars.

34

JONATHAN

*K*nock. *Knock.*

My knuckles make a gentle sound on Kiara's window. It's dark out, but we're used to this routine.

We're a month into the summer, and Kiara and I are up early to catch another sunrise. It's part of our pattern. We wake up early and find each other in the dark, our hands fumbling together at the trailhead. After the sun rises, we spend our days snapping photos of Legacy Inn and its guests — and sneaking in a few kisses in the meantime. At night? We lay on the beach, stare into the stars, and talk.

By now, I know this trail by heart. I understand where the bumps and ridges and tree roots lie.

Nonetheless, I always hold her hand as we hike. I pretend that I do it to make sure we don't get lost, but I really just love having her close to me.

The trail is slick after yesterday's rainfall, so we proceed slowly. By the time we get to the viewpoint, the sky is lightening. We continue to the summit and I feel thankful that the days are still long.

As we get closer to the summit, I hold back and wait for Kiara to stand next to me.

"Ready?" My voice is quiet. There's no one around, but I don't want to disturb the balance of this place.

She squeezes my hand in response.

One.

Two.

Three.

Together, we stride forward with our faces down. On the count of three, we raise our heads to take in the panoramic view. It's a little habit I suggested when Kiara teased that I was seeing the view before she was. This way, we get to experience the first look together.

"Not bad, golden boy," Kiara says.

It's a crisp and clear morning, and the horizon hints at what will be a colorful sunrise. Kiara sits, making herself comfortable on a large expanse of rock before taking out her camera and setting up. Then, she shivers.

"You okay?" I ask.

"Should've brought a warmer jacket."

I reach around my camera bag and find a to-go mug. "This'll help."

Kiara's eyes light up. "Good thinking."

Before knocking on her window this morning, I went to the kitchen and filled it with hot coffee. Fernando opened his mouth, but left his questions unasked, and simply smiled.

She takes a long swig and then curls further into her jacket, clutching the to-go mug with as much passion as she does her camera. I laugh and wrap my arms around her to keep her warm.

"You're gonna miss the views." She leans back against me, shamelessly stealing my body heat.

"It's worth it. We have many mornings to chase the sunrise."

I lie down on the rock so Kiara and I are curled together, watching the sky change colors. It's peaceful and we don't need to speak. Every once in a while, Kiara sits up and lifts the camera to her face. It's an epic sunrise.

Kiara lies down after taking a photo, and she fingers the bottom of my hoodie.

I burst out laughing. "Still cold?"

"The coffee helps." There's a smile in her voice. "I was just thinking that I love seeing you wear hoodies and shorts. You never wear stuff like that at school."

She trails off and her body stiffens. She's broken an unspoken rule. We don't talk about how things were at school, and we definitely don't talk about how things will be when we go back. Our rivalry is an ancient story, practically a Greek Legend. The Feud of Golden Boy and Kiara the Queen.

"You gotta admit the polo shirts and slacks are a popular look." I joke, but it doesn't have the desired effect. Kiara is still lying uncomfortably. "Coach tells us we need to wear polo shirts. Do our hair so we look professional. It's part of the image. But next year, I'm bringing back the hoodie."

"Good," Kiara says. "It's tough for a girl to steal a polo shirt."

I kiss the top of her head. "My hoodies are yours."

35

KIARA

*T*he ground moves under me and I groggily open my eyes.

"Ready?" Jonathan whispers into my ear.

I jerk awake. Somehow, between the beautiful sunrise, the early morning, and being cuddled into Jonathan's chest, I'd fallen asleep.

"How long was I out for?" I ask. The sun is far above the peaks. I peel myself off Jonathan.

"Only a day or two."

I punch him playfully. When he tries to block me, I leap, tackle him, and we roll in the dirt.

"I surrender!" He shouts, cradling his head. "It was only half an hour!"

"And you just let me sleep?"

He grips my wrists to stop me from attacking him. "You looked so peaceful, drooling and snoring and everything."

In horror, I put my hand to my face before realizing he's joking. I give him another swat and then stand up, wiping off my pants and jacket. "You think you're so funny."

When I look down at Jonathan, though, he's frozen. He's staring just behind me and motions for me to be quiet.

My heart slams in my chest. Bears?

Jonathan slowly stands, still staring at a point beyond my shoulder. His face is a mask of tense vigilance. Fear grips me and I can barely breathe.

He carefully walks towards me, side-stepping around me to get between me and the creature — whatever it is.

Very, very slowly, I turn around to see what he's staring at.

On the mountainside just beyond, there's a beautiful white mountain goat with three baby goats. I gasp and then hold my breath. The adult goat is looking at us, simultaneously bored and cautious.

There's the wildlife shot.

Slowly, I raise my camera to my face, capturing the sight of these four goats in the morning sunlight.

The group of goats strides along the rocks and around the corner, disappearing from sight.

Jonathan grabs my hand. "Unbelievable."

We make our way back to the trail, treading carefully down the mountain as the path is still slick. My stomach is in a ball of excitement thinking about how amazing the morning was. I'm going through the photos, wanting to relive it.

I click onto a sunrise photo. "This one's great. Check it out!"

For the shot, I'd zoomed in on the peaks across the lake and then used a darker setting on the camera to bring out the warm tones. The image perfectly contrasts the cool and warm features of the scene.

I lean towards Jonathan to show him the picture, and I immediately lose my footing.

The trail slides out from beneath me.

My stomach lurches.

I fly through the air.

Jonathan whips around, catches me before I hit the ground. "Didn't I tell you not to fall? Or drop your camera?"

"I believe you told me it was very expensive," I say. "But it's fine. I wasn't really falling. Just testing your reflexes."

He laughs and stands me up straight in front of him, his beautiful blue eyes gazing into mine.

I think I'm in love with you.

My heart stops.

Freaked, I jump out of his arms.

"Anyway, check it out!" My words tumble out as I try to shake off the feeling from moments ago.

Jonathan checks out the photo over my shoulder, his eyeing growing wide. "Garcia... that is really, really good."

"You *are* talking to a Queen here." I beam with pride, cradling the camera close to me.

"You should try again," he says.

"What?"

"The Glacier Journal. Send that photo to them."

I walk down the trail, stammering. "I don't think I have what they're looking for."

I was definitely not expecting him to say that. After my rejection letter, I never want to contact them again. They probably know me as that girl who takes lifeless and dull photos. Ugh, what a reputation.

Jonathan takes my hand. "It's an awesome shot, Kiara. What do you have to lose?"

Optimism fills his eyes, and it warms my heart that he believes in me this much.

"My dignity? My self-respect? *More* of my reputation?"

"Can't lose what you never had," he says, grinning. He

catches my hand before I can swat him. Stupid soccer player reflexes. "I'm serious," he says.

"About my lack of dignity?"

"About how good that photo is. I'd buy the Journal on that photo *alone.*"

I smile warmly. I've never had this kind of support before... It feels nice. Even though I'll no doubt get rejected, part of me wants to see the world like Jonathan sees it. Endless opportunities, everywhere.

"Okay, fine," I say, rolling my eyes. "You know I can't say no to that golden boy charm."

He leans down to kiss me, picking me up and wrapping me in his arms. As his lips meet mine, I can't deny it:

I love Jonathan Wright.

JONATHAN

"*Y*es!" Kiara dances in a circle as the last striped ball falls cleanly into a pocket.

She blows on the top of her pool cue like it's on fire and then walks around the table to stand next to me.

"Your butt's mine, golden boy." She grins and bumps her hip against mine. She bends over the table to hit the 8-ball and I hold my breath.

Clack.

The 8-ball narrowly misses the corner pocket.

Kiara glares at it.

"What was it you were saying about my butt, Garcia?" I ask with a sweet smile as I line up the cue to hit my last solid ball. I wait a moment, the perfect build-up of anticipation, before hitting the six ball into the pocket directly in front of her.

She rolls her eyes, leaning forward on the table. The game is heating up. The table is entirely cleared and only the 8-ball is left.

I chalk the end of my cue. The 8-ball is sitting against the far rail. The angle will be difficult, but not impossible.

"Scared, golden boy?"

I snort. "Of you?"

I bend over the table and take a deep breath.

I tap the ball with the end of the cue.

The cue ball clacks against the 8-ball, which rolls pathetically to a stop.

Kiara's turn. With a confident smirk, she grabs her pool cue and sits on the edge of the table, arranging the cue behind her back. Very smooth.

She lines up the final shot, and I smile looking at her concentrated expression. No matter what Kiara is doing, her face tells the whole story. I wish I could get a photo of her now.

It's the middle of July and the days at the Inn are filled with magic. There's another garden party tonight, and Kiara and I are dressed accordingly. Her hair is tied back into a ponytail and she's wearing one of her colorful dresses. She looks beautiful, as usual.

Without appearing to put an ounce of effort in, Kiara knocks the 8-ball into the pocket, winning the game. She does a little dance around the table.

I pretend to break my cue stick over my knee before putting it away.

She laughs and circles her arms around my neck. "Someone owes me a secret."

On our breaks and when guests aren't around, we've started playing pool in the games room. Kiara thought it'd be fun to raise the stakes and have the loser share a secret.

I have no complaints. I've learned that Kiara broke her arm while trying to walk in her mom's heels as a kid and *not* when she was skateboarding. I've learned that she loves mac and cheese because it's the only thing her father made when she was young. And I've learned that Sebastian, her cat at home, is the love of her life, and that no matter what I say or do, I will be a distant second. At best.

Kiara is constantly surprising me. I had no idea what to expect when I suggested we play a game of pool a month ago, but Kiara has proven herself to be a quick learner. She went from spilling all of her secrets to asking for mine in a few weeks.

I came prepared today. I have a secret that I'm excited to share with her.

"Okay." I'm lost in her eyes, as usual. "So, I've been thinking a lot lately..."

Her eyes change from blissfully curious to suddenly serious. Does she know what I'm about to say?

I exhale quickly, finally getting the words out. "I want to go to photography school."

Kiara laughs, a light and melodic sound. "That's an *awesome* idea!"

"Yeah," I say, feeling shy. "I've been thinking about it and I want to pursue photography as a career. It's because of you. You make it all seem possible."

The words rush out, and as I speak the truth, I feel lighter. I can finally see the world clearly and I know my path. Kiara and I sway back and forth to a silent tune, a melody we both dance to.

"I'm so happy to hear that," Kiara says, her excitement clear on her face. "You were meant to do photography."

"You think so?"

"You do have the beanie for it."

"The hat makes the artist," I say, laughing. Kiara always tells me the truth. If she doubted my ability, she'd say so.

"My grandpa was the only one who supported me doing photography. He was such a happy, optimistic guy." I glance at my camera, sitting on the edge of the pool table. "He's the one who got me the camera."

"He must've been a wonderful person."

"The best," I say. "That's why I skipped the game last fall to take photos. He always made me feel that I shouldn't be ashamed of what I want. I wish you could've met him."

Our swaying slows as Kiara stands on her tip-toes to give me a kiss. The air around us feels magnetic and I never want to let her go. Realization strikes—

I love her.

I've wanted to tell her for days now, but I've never been sure about the moment.

A commotion by the door causes us to jump apart. Anaya flings the door to the games room wide open, dragging Wes inside by the hand. "Okay, you two lovebirds, let's get moving. Other people want to play."

Without an ounce of concern for interrupting a tender moment, Anaya shoos us towards the porch.

Kiara and I break down in laughter, and I give Wes a fist-bump as we leave the games room.

The interruption was for the best; I don't want to scare her off by telling her too early.

37

KIARA

*W*es and Anaya have taken over the games room. I've noticed how cute they've been lately and I'm happy to give them the space. As Jonathan and I step onto the porch, he pokes me in the side and then bolts into the garden.

"I have one more thing to tell you!" He shouts over his shoulder as he runs. "But you have to catch me first!"

I dash after him down the stairs, my head still spinning with excitement from his confession. Jonathan Wright wants to go to photography school. Jonathan. Wright.

It's been a month and a half since we arrived at the Inn and I'm shocked by how much things have changed. The weeks have gone by in a blur and I've enjoyed work more than I could have imagined. At the end of the day, we have dinners together and then spend the evenings or afternoons exploring the grounds around the Inn.

Jonathan has this unbelievable ability to make any task fun. If I was a black and white still from the 50s, he'd be a colorful, wild image from the 70s. I never could have imagined how much fun *living* could be.

With him, it all comes so easily. Whether we're relaxing in the hammocks or climbing to the Legacy summit for sunrise, Jonathan and I are attached at the hip.

We did a very poor job hiding it from the other staffers, as Nath so loudly demonstrated one morning not long ago.

"Ki, I told you! Love and hate, two sides of the same coin," Nath said. I remembered one of the first things she said to me when I arrived at the Inn — that she didn't like her husband initially.

I blushed and scurried from the room, dragging a confused Jonathan with me.

What I've enjoyed most is sharing my passion for photography. When Jonathan arrived, I expected him to be terrible. I believed he didn't care about his position and that this whole summer was a big joke to him.

But he took it seriously. He's a fast learner, and I know he'll do great at photography school.

Even better?

My photos are improving, too. Enjoying the moments is helping me capture them.

I run as fast as I can and almost catch Jonathan.

He darts into the empty gazebo.

I fly around the corner, wrap my arms around his waist, and almost drag him to the ground. "You owe me a secret."

"A secret? Or is it more of a question? Hmm."

"A secret question? I'm intrigued."

He unwraps me from his waist and holds my hands tenderly. For a brief moment, he looks everywhere but my eyes, but then his gaze settles on me.

"You are, without a doubt, one of the most intelligent, inspiring, beautiful people I've ever known. You have changed my life."

My heart races and I blush furiously.

Jonathan takes a deep breath. "And now, I want to know…"

My heart is racing and my stomach is full of butterflies. What is he going to say?

"Will you be my girlfriend?"

My heart flutters in my chest, but I shrug like it's nothing. "Maybe."

Jonathan waits, his face anxious.

"I need you to promise me something first," I say. "And it's very important."

"Anything."

I pause, letting him sweat a little. "You let me have the bigger side of the hammock."

He lets out a tremendous sigh of relief. "I thought it was serious."

"Oh, it's deadly serious."

He laughs, takes me in my arms, and spins me in a circle. "For you? Anything."

His finger traces the side of my face, and he tilts my chin back. He kisses me, and I feel like I might explode with happiness.

I don't want the kiss to end, but real life intrudes.

"Jonathan! Kiara! We need you!"

We break apart, and I'm laughing harder than before at the thought of an angry Delia coming on the warpath.

Together, we head out of the gazebo, strolling back to the Legacy Inn, our hands locked tight.

38

JONATHAN

"*I*f you're dating Kiara the Queen, does that make you King Jonathan?"

I read Troy's email and roll my eyes. I told him in my last message that Kiara and I are officially together. Though I still haven't mentioned *why* I'm here at the Inn, I've told him *why* he should stop using the nickname.

I write a quick response to Troy, stressing that the nickname is old news and asking about things in Edendale. According to his last message, my secret is still safe — no one in Edendale suspects that I skipped out on Momentum.

In fact, a few of my friends and teammates have emailed asking about Momentum and about team tryouts for next year.

I also had an email from Lucas asking if I minded that he's now dating Isabella. I chuckled loudly at that and sent him my blessings.

Guilt crushes me, though, as I open my mom's email last.

I hope you're doing well at Momentum, Jonathan! Your dad and I know that you're giving it your best shot and we are so

proud of you. Let me know what the address is so I can send you
your care package. I've included lots of protein bars and new shin
guards!

Love, Mom

I can hear the tense note in her voice asking for the
address. I barely remember a time my parents *weren't* high-
strung and stressed about my soccer career.

I shake myself off and remember the soccer ball
currently wedged under Kiara's cabin. We tried to get it out
the other day, but it's truly stuck. That is the most effort I've
put into playing soccer this summer.

I click out of my mom's email without typing a response,
reminding myself not to feel guilty for pursuing my dream.
This summer has already been such a massive step forward
and I feel more excited every day to go to school for
photography.

I make my way out of the reception area and walk to the
garden. Kiara and I went back to Legacy summit this morning, and I decided to check my emails before work. Now, I'm
on duty and looking for Kiara.

She's at the docks, helping an elderly lady move her
sunchair away from the edge.

The past two months with Kiara have been amazing.
Sunshine, rain, thunderstorm — it doesn't matter, every day
feels magical. Her courage makes me brave and her
creativity inspires me. She would've loved my grandpa.

The last time we were at the computers, Kiara sent a
photo to the Glacier Journal. The image was spectacular; I
was so proud of her. She captured the sunrise perfectly, and
I have so much faith in her and in that photo.

I don't know if she's heard back yet, but she doesn't seem
concerned. If they don't accept the picture, I'll be shocked.

As I approach, Kiara looks up at me. With her breezy

smile and long hair, she looks perfect. I bring my camera to my face and snap two photos of her as she helps the elderly lady settle into the chair.

Most of my recent photos are of Kiara. I'm trying to capture her expressions and do her justice, but my photos don't compare to how beautiful she is in real life. I like to think a few of them are close, though.

She hops down from the dock and walks over. "Creeping me again?"

"Always."

We walk towards the Inn as I scroll back through my photos. It's incredible to see how they've changed. With Kiara's help, my photography skills are getting better and better. Not that I can share this with the people back home...

"Something's on your mind." Kiara says. A statement, not a question.

"My parents," I say hesitantly. "I wish they could see these."

Part of the reason I went to the computers was to see if I had any emails from my parents. We've always celebrated my victories together. It breaks my heart to pursue something I love without being able to share it with them.

Kiara gives me a hug, resting her head on my shoulder. "They'd be proud."

"Maybe," I say, but I doubt it.

"They would be. You have so much to be proud of."

I try to smile, but I still feel guilty.

Kiara turns to me as we enter the garden. Her beautiful eyes meet mine.

"And if nothing else, just know that *I'm* proud of you."

39

KIARA

"Kiara, Jonathan!" Bree bursts through the bushes.

It's a warm afternoon and I'm exhausted. Jonathan and I are regularly chasing the sunrise at the Legacy summit, and this means that our afternoon naps in the hammocks are key to our survival.

I sit up reluctantly, tired and bleary-eyed. In the hammock next to me, Jonathan is sitting upright with his hair standing on one side. He looks like an electrified meerkat. I stifle a snort as Bree approaches us.

"What's up?" I ask.

"Nice hair." Bree says to Jonathan. He hurriedly pats down the one side as I burst into laughter. "Have you heard from Delia? We're having a meeting tonight."

"Haven't seen her." I was looking forward to a long, blissful sleep.

"What time?" Jonathan yawns.

"She said she has a big announcement." Bree says. "Meeting's at six in the staff room."

"Cool," Jonathan draws out the "oo" as he flops back into his hammock.

I roll my eyes and hop out. It's almost 5:30 now, there's no point in trying to sleep anymore.

"I'll come with you, Bree." I say before turning towards Jonathan and uttering "sweet dreams" at his toppled self.

I detect a barely audible snore. Yep, he'll be out for a while.

Bree and I link arms as we head back towards the cabins. I appreciate her spontaneity and sense of humor. I think we might actually be friends at school in the coming year. She and I are so different, but Legacy Inn blurs the lines.

"See ya at six, Kiara." Bree heads off towards the lake, likely to find Noah.

I stare at my little A-frame home and make a quick decision to head to the computers.

I've been avoiding checking my emails. Ever since I sent Glacier Journal my sunrise photo, I've been having second thoughts as to whether it was the right choice. Not only for me, but for Jonathan. I don't expect to get a response, but I worry more about breaking the news to him than getting the rejection. He has so much faith and optimism, it'd be heartbreaking to see him disappointed in their response, or lack of response.

I'm walking through the reception to get to the computers when Delia calls out from the little office.

"Kiara, dear! Would you be able to give me a hand?"

I jog over and take a peek inside the office. Delia is trying and failing to grab an enormous cardboard box from the top of the cupboard. I grab one end of the box and almost topple beneath the weight.

"Woah, Delia!" I exclaim as I awkwardly maneuver part of the box into my hands. "You were going to do this alone?!"

Delia successfully grabs the other end of the box. "It's not *that* heavy."

Categorically untrue. We hoist the box off of the cupboard and place it on the ground. The top pops open, revealing stacks of the Inn's brochures — the same one I had on my dining table before coming to Legacy Inn.

"Thank you, dear." Delia shoves the box towards her desk.

Her office is cute, colorful, and no-nonsense. Photos of family and friends are scattered haphazardly on the walls, and Inn-related paperwork litters her desk. A felt garland hangs decoratively on the back of her door — a remnant from the Holiday season. Behind her desk, a massive aerial photo of the Inn and the grounds shows its age. The Inn has grown exponentially in the last few years.

"It's a good shot, isn't it?" Delia asks as I gaze at the aerial photo.

"How old is it? The Inn doesn't even have the guest wings."

"Ten, fifteen years, maybe?" Delia picks up a brochure and smacks it against her palm. "All of our photography is outdated. That's why I'm so glad to have you and Jonathan here."

"Same."

Delia chuckles, takes a seat at her desk, and rifles through a stack of paperwork. Anything she deems not important gets tossed to the floor.

"I had my reservations when this thing started. But look how far you two have come! You're friends, our social media accounts are blooming, and each picture is better than the next."

"He's getting better and better, isn't he?" I say, smiling.

I'm 'winning' the social media post competition, but Jonathan's catching up.

"Not just him, my dear." Delia finds the piece of paper she wants and scribbles something near the top. "You've always had technical talent. Any fool could see that from your application. But now your photos have that something special. You're not taking pictures, you're capturing life — if you'll excuse a sentimental old fool."

I blush, and my heart threatens to float from my chest. My photos are getting better — and it's not just me noticing.

Delia checks a clock on her desk. "Almost six. Time to head to the staff room. I've got a few announcements — one that you and Jonathan in particular will want to hear. I'll see you there."

I leave Delia's office walking on air. Not only does she believe that Jonathan and I are doing good work, but she also implied that my photos are *alive* — the very aspect that Glacier Journal said I needed to work on.

I want to run to the computers right away to see if they've responded. Has my sunrise photo been accepted?

But I know the announcement has to come first. I vow to check my email after hearing what Delia has to say.

40

JONATHAN

*M*y phone alarm pulls me out of my blissful sleep. I stretch out in the hammock and grunt. Ugh, can't I just have five more minutes?

The answer? No. I barely have time to run over to the Inn for Delia's announcement.

I sit up groggily and pat my hair down, remembering Kiara's laugh earlier. I exit the hammock and jog towards the Inn. By the time I get to the staff room, everyone is happily milling about. I spot Nath and Vin across the room and make my way over. Kiara is nowhere to be seen, but she's likely going to be late anyway.

"Hey guys!" I exclaim as I approach them. "Do you know what this is about?"

Nath smiles, turning to Vin. "Should we tell him?"

"Delia swore me to secrecy."

Vin and Nath laugh, and their cryptic answer tugs at my curiosity.

A hush comes over the room as Stefi walks in with Cooper Monroe. I'd gotten to know the guy over the summer and he seems pretty cool. His dad hasn't been around much — too busy filming, probably. I give Cooper a nod from across the room, and he smiles back. He always looks like he's laughing at something.

Kiara finds me in the crowd, and her hand slips into mine. "Golden boy."

Her smile is the biggest I've ever seen it. She wraps her arms around me and I kiss the top of her head. It feels like I missed something.

Delia steps up onto a chair at the front of the room. "I imagine you're wondering why I brought you here on such short notice."

The staff room goes quiet, save for the tapping of feet in the room next door as guests grab their dinners.

Delia beams, her bright smile energizing the room. "A few quick announcements to share."

"What do you think it is?" Kiara whispers.

Delia goes on a tangent about the success of the Inn and how we're welcoming our millionth guest today.

"Maybe they're expanding?" I whisper.

Truthfully, I have no idea. The only thing I know is that I don't want things to change. I love Legacy Inn the way it is. It might be selfish of me, but it's the truth.

"Given our success, we have decided that it's time to revamp the 'look' of the Legacy Inn. I don't mean the actual construction and design — I'm sure you all remember the renovations that took place two summers ago—"

A frustrated groan travels through the room.

"It wasn't THAT bad," Delia says.

"I still have nightmares," Vin replies.

"Quiet, you." Delia waves Vin away. "We've decided that it's the *perfect* time to launch a brand-new Legacy Inn advertising campaign! And who better to headline this campaign than our two star student photographers?"

Kiara's hand drops from mine as everyone looks our way. My mouth pops open. What is she saying?

"We love the work Jonathan and Kiara have been doing around the Inn and on the Legacy Inn social media accounts. We want to use one of YOUR photos to headline the entire campaign! This photo will be featured on our biggest ad yet and will be shown around the world."

My heart stops and I look over at Kiara. Her face is frozen, her mouth in a tight line as she stares at Delia.

Only *one* of us will get this chance?

This is an amazing opportunity. Headlining an ad like this means international exposure for our work. It's exactly what Kiara is looking for, and it's also a major opportunity for me to add to my portfolio and get into photography school.

Delia wraps up her announcements, but I can't hear a word she says. My ears are ringing as a billion things run through my mind. I'm vaguely aware that Kiara hasn't moved a muscle either, our hands hanging limply by our sides.

Staffers leave the room, congratulating us as they go, and I offer a weak smile of thanks.

The staff room clears and I finally muster the courage to turn to Kiara. Her eyes are stormy and unsure. I open my mouth to say something, but I have nothing to say.

Both of us want this more than anything.

But only one of us will get it.

41

KIARA

*O*nce again, Delia takes the cake with her shocking announcements. My thoughts are dark and dejected as I consider her words.

I'm in competition with the boy I love.

Only one of us will headline the international ad campaign.

It's everything I've ever wanted. Everything I need if I want to get out of Edendale. But it comes with the highest cost imaginable — for me to win, Jonathan must lose.

"I need to clear my head," I say abruptly. Jonathan doesn't reply. He feels very far away.

I make my way to the computers, emotions raging through me. I felt so encouraged after my meeting with Delia, and I couldn't wait to tell Jonathan. I was going to invite him to be there with me when I checked my emails for a response from Glacier Journal.

Then Delia made the announcement, and the world crashed down.

Headlining a campaign like this is all I've ever wanted. This would be the *perfect* step on my path out of Edendale.

And yet, I know what this would mean to Jonathan. He wants to pursue photography in school, and this opportunity would make him a shoo-in for *any* photography program.

So, what should I do? My feelings for Jonathan are real, but can I sacrifice this incredible opportunity — and therefore my future — for him?

I spend minutes sitting in front of the blank computer screen with my head in my hands. I try to reel in the weight of my emotions.

Get it together, Kiara.

I sign in and scroll past the unread emails on the screen, holding my breath. My stomach is in knots.

But I come up with nothing. There is still no response from Glacier Journal.

I curse to myself, wishing that I hadn't gotten my hopes up.

I click onto an email from Ava, her cheerful tone and cute stories from band camp soothing me. I haven't told her I'm dating Jonathan, and now I'm not sure what to say. I click out of her email without replying. I can't muster enough cheer for the happy response I know she wants.

Then, I spot an email from my mom. I've emailed her once since I've been here and it looks like she finally replied.

Hey, Kiki. I'm glad to hear that you're enjoying yourself at Legacy Inn. But, you're right, this is an INCREDIBLE step towards your career. Shoot for the stars and remember your bright future. The end of summer will come quickly and you'll be so happy to have this experience under your belt. I know you've got this covered, hun.

Love, Mom.

Her words are a bucket of ice water poured over my head.

She's right. I need to focus on my future. That's why I'm here at the Legacy Inn this summer — to work. I remember her words — there's no time for love if you're not doing what you love. Have I lost track of my path?

I log off of the computer without replying. I have no news for her, except that I'm now aiming for an even bigger and brighter opportunity. I only have a month before the end of summer, I have to take advantage of every minute.

The event room is bustling as guests enjoy their dinners, but I'm numb to it all. I head out into the garden, contemplating the amount of work I need to do to ensure that this summer pays off.

A pang of shame hits me as I realize that I don't have my camera with me. Dread washes over me.

Have I totally compromised my future?

42

JONATHAN

"Kiara, you home?" I wait patiently outside of her door.

Nothing but silence.

I head back towards the Inn, my stomach flipping over. She's gone again, I guess.

My sense of unease grows with each step down the gravel path.

As though she can read my mind, Nath calls to me from the garden. "Hey Jonathan, have you seen Kiara?"

"I haven't."

"Now where did she run off to, you think?" Nath shakes her head, and I get the impression she knows how I'm feeling.

"Wish I knew."

It's been ages since Kiara and I spent time together. Lately, it's like she's never at her cabin. I've tried to chat with her at work, but she's distant and disengaged. Our sunrise hikes are different now too. She's quiet and distracted the entire time, and she's been canceling regularly.

When I do see her, she's buried behind her camera. She

won't go anywhere without it and stresses about getting the "perfect" photo. Because of this, we rarely explore the grounds anymore. Instead of sitting by the lake or napping in the hammocks, Kiara opts to hang out in the garden or around the docks — near the guests.

The months we spent together feel like a distant memory.

I tried to talk to her about the headlining campaign after Delia's announcement. She caught up with me outside the garden, a grim smile on her face.

"Hi."

"That was intense," I said, exhaling. "How're you feeling?"

She smiled, but she seemed distracted. "Good, I guess. You?"

"Good." I grabbed her hands, but they hung limply in mine. "I know we both want this headlining thing really badly, but I still want to be with you. This summer has been incredible. There has to be a way we can figure this out. Maybe Delia can feature us both? Or maybe we work together to get a photo to headline the campaign? What do you think?"

I waited quietly for her response. As much as I wanted the campaign, I also wanted to be with Kiara. The last two months felt like breathing fresh air after a lifetime of being trapped inside.

"Yeah, maybe," she said. She wouldn't meet my eyes.

I gave her a big hug, hoping we were on the same page, but unable to ignore the doubts creeping through the shadows.

It's been a week since that conversation. A week since she started pulling away and pushing herself back into her photography. I notice the stress on her face during the garden parties. She doesn't chat with the guests anymore, and she obsesses over getting the ideal shot by the gazebo.

It's been my mission lately to get her out of her funk.

And that means it's time for a prank.

When I knocked on her door, my plan was to bring her back to the canyon where we cliff jumped. With all the extra time I've had on my hands, I've crafted a convincing, life-sized cardboard cutout of Kade Monroe using his headshot.

Delia was curious to know why I was using all the spare cardboard in her office, but I couldn't tell her. I didn't want it to risk it getting back to Kiara.

I set up the cardboard cutout by our perch in the canyon. I couldn't wait to see Kiara's face when she spotted Kade popping out of a bush.

"Jonathan!" Delia calls out from the porch as I make my way through the garden, wrapped up in my thoughts. "Would you be a dear and help Vin with the huppah? He's in the games room trying to lift it himself. I keep telling him he's not as young as he once was — the rate he's going he'll break his back."

"Sure thing." I walk through the garden to the games room, and there I spot Vin hidden behind the intricately ornate huppah.

He struggles to drag it along the floor -- but he's only made it to the pool table. He breathes heavily, resting among the flowers tied delicately to one of the poles.

On my approach, he whips the flowers out of his face. "When I offered to help Delia, she told me I just needed to move some flowers. This wasn't what I had in mind."

I grin. "Let me help."

"Thanks, Jonathan."

I lift one end of the huppah and Vin takes the other.

"One of the last weddings of the season, and it's the only

one that requires such an unwieldy — albeit beautiful — canopy. Here I thought I got away without having to move this ridiculous thing all summer."

"You must've jinxed yourself."

We pivot the huppah as we struggle through a doorway. I can't believe that the end is almost here. In just three weeks, I'll be back home, facing my parents, and away from Kiara. My heart falls and I almost drop the huppah.

"Got it?" Vin asks, panic in his voice.

"Sorry."

We maneuver the canopy down the steps of the porch. After finally installing it at the far end of the garden, Vin stands next to me, and wipes the sweat from his brow.

"I can hardly believe it," he says between breaths. "It'll be a fun wedding. I've got to hand it to you, Jonathan. You and Kiara have both taken some spectacular photos over the summer. I hope you can relax and have a good time."

He's right, I need to take advantage of this time with Kiara. She's been so distant lately; it'll be great to spend some time together again.

I look out over the wedding decorations throughout the garden, trying to commit the scene to memory. And yet, there's a familiar feeling of unease. At every big event this summer, I've dreaded seeing one of my close friends or family members. I've been lucky to this point, no one I know has come to the Inn. But I know that Isabella's cousin is getting married this summer, and she's Jewish.

What are the chances? I shake myself off and the feeling of dread disappears.

I'm probably just uneasy about the situation with Kiara. Seriously, what are the chances?

43

KIARA

I add the finishing touch to my outfit for the evening — a white ribbon to tie back my hair.

I assess the final product in the mirror and feel satisfied. My little black dress has been the key to surviving the parties and events at the Inn this summer. Likely because it can be worn in a myriad of ways.

Tonight, I'm wearing it halter-style, with my hair elegantly swept into a half-ponytail. Since arriving at the Inn, my ability to dress up has improved. I've tried out a few different hairstyles and I've worn all of my dresses and skirts at least once. I'd laugh to see my mom's face now. While I won't say that I *enjoy* wearing dresses, I don't hate them anymore.

I apply a touch of mascara and lip gloss before placing my camera around my neck to complete the ensemble. It's as good as it's gonna get.

I sigh as I open the door to my cabin. It's one of the last ceremonies of the season and, so, one of my last chances to capture wedding magic at the Inn.

These past ten days have felt like a lot of work, especially compared to how I spent the first two months at Legacy Inn. I've captured an endless amount of photos, taking advantage of the golden hours at sunrise and sunset. I've thought of little else. I take my meals to-go to ensure I don't miss out on any photo ops.

It's been especially difficult seeing the strain with Jonathan. A large part of me *wants* to spend time with him, I wish we could talk and hang out as we used to do. But I have other obligations and those need to come first.

I'm excited for the wedding tonight. Hopefully, we'll be able to catch up once we're done shooting photos.

I jog along the gravel pathway leading to the garden. Delia asked me to take photos of the bridal party before the wedding, and I jumped at the opportunity. Unfortunately, in true Kiara fashion, I'm running late.

The garden looks beautiful when I arrive — there's white tulle everywhere and an exquisite huppah at the front of the aisle. It will be a stunning wedding. I get a couple of photos of the garden in wedding-preparation mode and then head to one of the massive guest rooms.

I take a deep breath and reach for the door handle, intending to quietly walk into the room and introduce myself without a fuss. The bride is usually freaking out around now; I don't want to add to the chaos.

The door pops open before I turn the handle, and I come face to face with someone I know very well.

Isabella Hall. Head cheerleader and Jonathan's ex-girlfriend.

She raises her eyebrows. "I know you. Edendale High, right?"

My voice sticks in my throat. I was not expecting Isabella — or anyone else from Edendale — to be a guest here. It's like opening a box of cake and finding a toad. I don't necessarily dislike her, but she comes from the ruling class of high school. And, historically, that class has not been friendly to me.

"Kiara." For some bizarre reason, I offer her my hand.

She doesn't take my hand, instead choosing to stare at my face, frowning, waiting for that spark of recognition. And then it comes.

"Kiara the Queen!"

I wince. Coming from Jonathan, the nickname is playful banter. From Isabella, it's poison.

Isabella opens the door wide. The entire bridal party is facing me.

Isabella bows. "Allow me to introduce your Majesty, Queen Kiara. Dressed for the royal ball and everything." Isabella wears a smile that doesn't reach her eyes.

My face turns red.

Isabella brushes past me, throwing her hair over her shoulder. "I'm off to the garden — but don't take too many photos without me."

Horribly embarrassed, I walk hesitantly into the room.

The bridal party stares, the bride, in particular, looking confused.

My face is undoubtedly a shade of red that beets would be proud of. I tentatively hold up my camera. "I'm the photographer?"

My words break the spell, and the room explodes into chatter. Thankfully, no one looks my way or acknowledges me. I commit myself to the job and wander through the room, taking photos as everyone gets ready for the big event.

When Isabella returns to the room, I make a conscious effort to avoid her.

"Okay, now let's try fake laughing!" I call out to the group in front of the gazebo.

The bridesmaids and groomsmen look at each other awkwardly and then force a laugh. But I know what comes next — the fake laughter quickly turns into genuine laughter. I capture the photos and smile.

I've been down by the gazebo taking portraits for a while now. This must be the twentieth photo of this group alone.

The entire wedding party has come down to the gazebo in bursts for their portraits. We had the bride and groom, the groomsmen, the bridesmaids, the parents, the family, and everyone else. I tick off the standard wedding checklist in my head. I've gotten used to this routine this summer.

Oddly enough, one person seems to be missing from this set of photos. Isabella Hall.

She was all over me to get photos of her as the bridal party was heading down to the garden. She wanted photos of herself alone, seated at the makeup table, sitting on one of the couches, looking out the window... The list was endless. But now that there are group photos, she has disappeared.

Not that I'm complaining. Isabella has an unnerving way of laughing at me without directly making fun of me. It's like everything she says is an inside joke I'm not a part of.

As the wedding party dissipates and everyone moves back to the garden, I think back to Isabella's words when we were in the guest suite taking photos.

"He's going to *love* these."

She said this over and over, going so far as to grab my camera to look back over the shots.

Who was she referring to? As I try to push away the

lingering curiosity, I can't ignore the slight feeling of unease. Somehow, over the summer, I forgot about the elite Edendale clique. And, perhaps worse, I forgot that Jonathan is a key part of that group. For a time, he and Isabella were heading it up.

According to Edendale High's gossip sources, Isabella and Jonathan broke it off in the spring. But people change their minds. Could she want him back?

And does he ever want her back? The thought feels toxic and dread overwhelms over me. The whole summer, we lived in a bubble, just the two of us. But now the bubble has popped. Does he think about her?

No. I know better than that. He asked me on that amazing date; he asked me to be his girlfriend. There's no way that meant nothing.

I approach the garden, smiling. We've had such a great summer. And now that the gazebo portraits are out of the way, it's just a matter of taking a few garden pictures and we'll be able to hang out for the rest of the evening.

But first, water.

I walk into the garden and head in the direction of the bar.

The garden is breathtaking, a scene from a fairytale. Slow music starts, lanterns emit a soft yellow light, and flowers are scattered through the space. People sway to the song, smiling, laughing.

I wander over to the bar, but Randy is nowhere to be seen. I sneak behind the counter and grab a glass from below, filling it quickly.

I sip my water and look over the crowd. Where's Jonathan?

I know he's probably wearing his black polo shirt and slacks. He calls it his wedding uniform.

A flash of blonde hair catches my eye as Isabella twirls around the dance floor. I roll my eyes at her dramatic spins. She's laughing gently and gets close to her dance partner, leaning in flirtatiously. She wraps her arms around him comfortably, an enormous smile on her face.

I squint to see who she's dancing with — perhaps it's the guy she was referring to earlier when I was taking her photo?

Who is your date tonight, Isabella Hall? Who is this mystery man?

The guy spins her around and my heart stops in my chest.

Jonathan.

The blood drains from my face and I'm frozen as he spins her again and dips her. She's leaning into him, close against his chest. As they dance, her eyes closed, reality slaps me across the face.

Jonathan and Isabella.

They're together.

Dread and shame consume me as I watch them pushed together, swaying happily. The rose-colored glasses have lifted and I'm left with harsh reality: I am a complete idiot.

If they're together, that means that our hang-outs meant nothing. It was stupid of me to think that they did. He was just using me for my photo knowledge. Was there any truth to any of his words?

"Woah, Kiara, you okay?" Randy's voice is blurred through the ringing in my ears.

I'm frozen in my shock, desperately wanting to disappear. I believed him.

Randy places her hand on my arm and gives me a light shake, bringing me back to life.

"I'm not feeling well." My voice sounds far away. "I think

I might go back to my cabin. Would you mind telling Delia that I'm sick?"

"Sure." Randy says and I almost want to look at her, but I wouldn't dare.

I'm sure she's seen Jonathan and Isabella together. She's probably taking pity on me for ever thinking he could care about me.

I abruptly turn away and leave the bar, rushing through the garden as the slow song ends.

When I reach the darkness of the lawn just beyond, I break into a run.

44

JONATHAN

*T*he sunlight beams in through the window, waking me up. I rub my eyes, knowing already that there are deep, dark circles under them.

I did not sleep well.

The wedding last night was beautiful. The decorations were sweet and everyone looked great. The DJ was surprisingly good, and I had an awesome time dancing with Randy, Vin, and the kids from school.

However, I didn't get to dance with the one person I wanted to dance with the most — Kiara.

I saw her earlier in the evening as she went down to the gazebo and I literally stopped and stared. She looked amazing. Her hair was half up and her dress showed off her curves perfectly. I could not wait to spend the evening laughing and dancing with her. I was going to take her to the canyon as soon as we could get a moment away.

Last night, I also wanted to ask her if she'd still be my girlfriend when we get back to Edendale High. If I've learned anything this summer, it's that I feel my absolute best when I'm with her.

Unlike with Isabella.

I sigh as I think back to the minutes that I had to dance with her last night. She looked hot, everyone could see that — Isabella always looks hot. But I felt nothing close to what I feel for Kiara.

It shocked me when Isabella came to me right after the wedding ceremony. I was checking something on my camera when she stopped in front of me.

"Hey babe," she said in her sultry low voice. I knew immediately who it was, and I plastered a fake smile on my face — she calls *everyone* babe.

"Isabella." I looked up from my camera, my heart sinking.

It was just my luck — one of the last events at the Inn and Isabella showed up. I didn't want anyone from my friend group to see me here. But Isabella? She's the worst one.

Isabella did her obnoxious two-cheek kissing thing. "I wasn't expecting to see you! What are you doing here? Aren't you meant to be at Momentum?"

"Ah yeah, I'm just..."

I tried to think of an excuse, anything to keep her off my trail. But nothing came to mind. My eyes darted around the area, looking for an escape. Kiara was standing over by Randy, taking a photo of guests at the bar. She was laughing and smiling, and a sense of calm came over me.

It was time to tell the truth.

"I'm a photographer here," I said, focusing back onto Isabella.

Her mouth popped open in shock as she looked me up and down. "Oh wow. Wait until Lucas hears about this!"

My resolve crashed around me. Lucas could not know about this, especially not now. I'd never hear the end of it.

"Please, don't tell anyone," I said, not bothering to disguise the panic in my voice. "Not yet. Everyone back home thinks I'm at Momentum. I need to be the one to break it to them."

I pictured the disappointment in my parents' faces. Not only would they be disappointed, but also betrayed. We weren't close as a family, not anymore, but that didn't mean they deserved to find out I was lying through Edendale's rumor mill. I needed to tell them myself.

"Seriously. Please." My voice was low and urgent.

Isabella grinned like a cat that cornered a mouse. If you wanted to ask a favor from Isabella, the price was always the same: your soul.

"Maybe I can keep your secret, Jonathan. Depends on what you can do for me." She traced her finger along my chest and I resisted the urge to step back. She glanced towards the tables by the dance floor, her voice dropping to a whisper. "See the guy over there? The one with the gorgeous blue jacket?"

He was tall, dark, and obviously athletic. He had a beard and dark hair cut close to his head. He was wearing sunglasses and looked effortlessly cool.

In other words, Isabella's type.

"His name's Mason, he's a freshman at Montana State," Isabella whispered and then abruptly turned away as Mason glanced our way. She leaned further into me. "I've been trying to catch his eye all night, but he's playing hard to get. I have a feeling I need to make him a little jealous. Catch what I'm saying?"

She stepped back and winked at me before adjusting the collar on my polo shirt.

My lips were in a thin line. I wanted this conversation to end as soon as possible.

Isabella smiled. "If you dance with me for one slow song to make him jealous, I'll keep your little secret."

The air rushed out of my lungs as my gaze flew to Kiara. She was chatting with the wedding party, heading towards the gazebo. I didn't want her to worry, and I figured one dance with Isabella wouldn't hurt.

And then I remembered something. "Wait, aren't you dating Lucas?"

Isabella rolled her eyes as she fingered my tie. This time, I couldn't hold back. I grabbed her hand and placed it firmly by her side.

"It's basically over," she simpered. Then, she spoke loud enough for Mason to hear. "I'll find you later, handsome. Then we can have that dance."

I stare at my tired face in the bathroom mirror as I brush my teeth. I'll say one thing for our relationship — Isabella never failed to surprise me. Moving on from Lucas without letting him know? That's a move straight out of her playbook.

Should I email him? He deserves to know, doesn't he?

My heart sinks as I consider seeing him in person. The thought of spending the next year in the Eagles' shadow sounds miserable. Troy is one of my best friends, but neither of us gets along with everyone on the team. In the past, we all hung out together because it was natural. It made sense. Everyone at school sees us as the 'Edendale Eagles', so of course we would spend all our time together.

After a summer away, going back to that life seems tiresome. I don't want to return to the confining cage that surrounds my MVP status — I got a glimpse of it with Isabella last night, and I didn't like it.

I leave the bathroom block and walk back to my cabin, my thoughts returning to Kiara.

She disappeared at the wedding; I never saw her come back from the gazebo. I spent the night taking photos of the guests and then, when things were winding down, I did some dancing with the staff. But my mind was on her.

At one point, I asked Randy and Nath if they'd seen her and Randy said that she wasn't well. I returned to the cabins soon after and knocked on her door, but there was no answer.

Something must be wrong. There's an icy chill coming from her cabin, it feels like the first wind of fall, and I definitely don't like it.

As if on cue, Kiara exits her cabin and steps onto her balcony. She glances my way and a look of disdain crosses her face. She wants nothing to do with me. A shiver runs down my spine.

"Kiara? Wait!"

She pretends she can't hear me, running down the gravel path.

My heart sinks. Do I go after her?

I climb the steps to my cabin and quickly change into work-appropriate clothes.

Did something happen at the wedding last night? My thoughts churn as I hurry down the path towards the Inn, holding my camera anxiously.

In the last few days since Delia's announcement, instead of working together, Kiara has been slipping away.

What if she decided that she doesn't want to work with me? What if she's thinking I'll hold her back? Maybe the reason she's been pulling away is because I haven't been doing a good enough job?

The world falls around me as the very same self-doubt

that I usually feel about soccer creeps over me. But this time, it's worse. Photography is something I *want* to do, not a pressure put on me by my parents and friends. If I've sacrificed my summer for photography and it doesn't work out, what does that mean for my future?

Maybe I read Kiara all wrong — maybe her excitement for me to go to photo school was because she thinks I'm not good enough to even be working here.

Maybe I can't do this.

My chosen path crumbles before me. I turn away from the Inn, walking towards the lake. For the first time ever, I have absolutely no appetite.

I hold my camera loosely in my hand as I walk along the path by the lake. I won't be taking photos today.

45

KIARA

I run all the way to the Inn, trying to put as much space as possible between Jonathan and I. I can't bear to hear his voice or see his face after what happened last night.

When I saw Jonathan dance with Isabella, I returned to my cabin and collapsed into a ball of tears. I was filled with regret, thinking about every wrong decision I made this summer. Not only did I forsake my photography and possibly ruin my chances at the future of my dreams, but I also fell for the *one* person I should never have even considered.

Jonathan fricking Wright. I can't believe I thought I loved him, I can't believe I kissed him.

As I tried to fall asleep, all I could see was Isabella's smiling face, Jonathan dipping her, the two of them so close together. It was like watching a nightmare unfold. Did he tell her my secrets? Did he tell her it was all a big front?

I was overcome by shame and embarrassment thinking about my confession about being rejected from Glacier

Journal. It's all ammo... He's just going to use that against me next year, and he likely has already told Isabella.

What nasty nickname will they come up with? Will they ditch "Kiara the Queen" for something far more shameful?

I imagined an alternate universe where I did exactly what I should've done this summer. In that reality, I ignored Jonathan and avoided him at all costs. I would've hiked alone to see the sunrise and taken photos of the guests alone. I didn't need him.

I don't need anyone.

At one point, I thought I heard a knock on my door, but it was likely just my mind reminding me to get back on track. I hope it isn't too late.

On autopilot, I stroll into the staff room and say hi to Fernando. I'm lost in thought when he physically steps in to stop me as I spread relish on my bagel instead of avocado.

"Is that a new recipe, mi bella?" Fernando looks at me skeptically.

I clue into the bottle of relish I'm holding and force a laugh. "Just something I'm trying."

I meant to put avocado on it, but clearly my head isn't on right.

I give Bree, Stefi and Anaya a wave as I walk out of the staff room with my weird relish bagel, opting to sit on the balcony. The breezy morning air is far more welcoming than the thought of seeing Jonathan in the staff room.

I gaze out at the lake absentmindedly. The surface is rippling and distorted this morning, and the peaks overhead are clouded and grey. It will be a cool day, the first hint of the end of summer. I wrap my cardigan tighter around my shoulders.

Have I jeopardized my future by having fun this summer?

As soon as I saw Jonathan and Isabella dancing together, I realized just how far off track I've gone. We only have a few weeks left at the Inn and I can't waste another minute. Especially not with Edendale's golden boy.

Jonathan was using me. He's here to win the competition and go back to Edendale High as a winner, just as he always does.

My heart turns icy as a feeling of betrayal sets in. I was an idiot to think he was ever a nice guy. I won't make that mistake again.

46

JONATHAN

*I*t's way past lunchtime when I finally make my way back to my cabin. I didn't have much of an appetite this morning, but I am *starved* right now.

I'm also filled with a stubborn determination.

I spent a large part of the morning skipping rocks into the lake. The ripples of the water consumed the rocks as I threw them, an oddly mesmerizing sight. It's a cooler day, and I regretted not grabbing my hoodie.

I need to talk to Kiara and find out what happened. Does she really think I'm not good enough? It doesn't sound like her. I never got the impression that she felt that way over the summer. But I could be wrong.

It wouldn't be the first time I disappointed someone.

My parents' and friends' expectations press on my shoulders as I consider going back to school in a few weeks. But the thought of disappointing Kiara? That seems worse.

The cabins loom gloomily in the distance as I jog over, ready to grab my hoodie and go straight to the Inn. As I approach, however, I spot Kiara walking towards the cabins.

"Kiara!" I break into a run, trying to catch her before she can disappear. "Wait. Please."

She does. But something is wrong. Her eyes burn and her face twists into a glare. "What now, golden boy?"

Her voice hits me like a shard of ice and my stomach drops. The way she says 'golden boy' is no longer playful. Now, she says it like it leaves an awful taste in her mouth.

"I just want to talk," I say. "Did I do something wrong?"

She rolls her eyes, keeping her distance. Her hair is pulled tight into a bun, her eyes vaguely swollen. I want to give her a hug, but that might set her off more.

"I had a future before you distracted me," she says. "A goal. A dream. We don't all skate through life getting everything we want handed to us. Some of us have to work our entire lives to be a photographer. Not that you'd understand. Not that it's something you'll ever do."

Her words are a punch to my gut. My heart plummets and I have trouble catching my breath. After everything we did this summer, all the time we spent together, the truth about what she really thinks of me is revealed. Being a professional photographer is not something I'll ever do unless it gets handed to me.

How long has she felt like this?

Are my photos actually good, or am I lying to myself?

Maybe everyone was trying to appease me. Maybe no one thought my work was any good. Maybe they wanted to fire me but it was too late.

My biggest fear has always been that, when the game is on the line, I'll fail to deliver. But now something bigger — my entire future — is on the line, and the person I love doesn't think I can do it. It's a worse pain than I could have imagined.

"I really hope you and Isabella are happy. You're so perfect together."

Her words blur. What does Isabella have to do with this? I open my mouth to ask what she means, but before I can, she closes it with a figurative uppercut.

"Leave me alone, golden boy. You've ruined enough."

Kiara storms into her cabin and the lock clicks shut.

47

KIARA

*T*ears sting my eyes as I slam the door and disappear into the comforting darkness of my cabin.

Crying over a boy twice in 24 hours is *way* too much. I sit on my bed, fingering the blanket as my pitiful tears fall. I told myself to be strong, to face Jonathan bravely. I don't know whether that came across. I ran away before I broke down.

Every word I said was true. When I came to Legacy Inn, my path was so clear — take photos, build my portfolio, get out of Edendale.

But now, it might be too late. I can't imagine a world where this summer was a step *back* instead of a step forward.

The thought of having to stay in Edendale past my graduation next year feels like a stab to the gut, especially now. My dream has always been to leave right after senior year. If my portfolio isn't good enough, can I get a job? Sticking around Edendale to add to my portfolio before I'm able to move to California or Barbados or Brazil is *not* part of the plan.

Bitterness fills me as I think of Edendale High's golden boy. Jonathan has had everything given to him. Including me. I sold out and handed myself to him on a silver platter. I taught him everything he needs to know to create a solid portfolio. All the advice and tips I gave him, that's all he needed me for. All he wanted me for.

Because of me, he'll continue living his golden life without having to lift a finger. I was right about that too — he'll never *have* to work hard. His life is easy and his dreams come true, no sweat involved.

An unwelcome whisper reminds me that my photos improved, too, through our collaboration, but I can't wrap my mind around that right now. I only know one thing to be true at this moment.

"I was right. Jonathan Wright can't be trusted." My voice breaks along with my heart.

How could I have thought I loved him? How could I have been so stupid as to think that maybe he loved *me*?

My tears dry on my face and my anger fuels determination. I have three weeks left here. I wipe away the memory and reapply some mascara with my goal set in my mind.

I will win this competition, and I will build a portfolio that secures my future. Jonathan was a detour, a small bump in the road. There's no time for love if you're not doing what you love.

And it's not too late until *I* decide it's too late.

48

KIARA

"Kiara?"

A distant voice calls, but I can't register the words. I'm lost in thought and in the distorted image of the world outside.

The rain falls hard onto the windows of the event room. The droplets gather in rivulets on the glass, creating a magical running image. The fog hangs low over the trees, swallowing the peaks at the far end of the lake.

I should get outside and take some photos. Back home, I loved this weather. The moody scenery creates the most emotional pictures.

"Kiara?" The voice is clearer, closer now. It snaps me out of my thoughts. "Earth to Kiara! Can you please take some pictures of Mr. and Mrs. van Nispen?"

I whirl around to face Bree and the two van Nispens. They're an elderly couple, very stately and nicely groomed. Well-traveled, probably.

"It's their 45th anniversary today. How about some photos to commemorate it?" Bree's voice is light, but her face is concerned.

"On it," I respond, embarrassed. I set up my camera as Bree strides off.

"Where are you two from?" I ask, a habit left over from my days spent with Jonathan. I paste a smile onto my face as I direct them to the front of the room where the lighting is better.

"The Netherlands." Mr. van Nispen answers with a hint of an accent.

Now, a genuine smile crosses my face as I ask them questions about the Netherlands. It's one of my top spots to visit when I finally travel the world.

Mr. and Mrs. van Nispen stand together comfortably, looking peaceful. They're like the quintessential happy couple, two puzzle pieces that fit together perfectly.

"So, 45 years." I line up the photo. "That's awesome, congratulations! What's your secret?"

Mr. van Nispen's rather stern expression softens as he looks at his wife. I quietly capture another photo as they gaze at each other with loving expressions.

"I can't leave her now. She knows too many secrets. She'd turn me in."

"Don't worry, dear, your secrets aren't that interesting."

He laughs. "And that's why I married her — she's never afraid to tell me the truth. Even when I don't want to hear it."

Mrs. van Nispen blushes, laughing easily.

"And I would never *dare* leave him. He makes me laugh. It keeps me young!"

I laugh along with the couple, capturing every moment of their loving expressions.

We finish, and my mind wanders back to Jonathan. Something about their answers stuck with me. Jonathan never failed to make me laugh. He showed me a side of myself that *could* be young and carefree.

Mr. and Mrs. van Nispen have been together for 45 years. The number seems impossible, so hard to imagine. I wish that Jonathan and I could've talked to them together. He's always got the best questions and the funniest jokes.

My heart sinks. It's been six days since we spoke to each other, and we've done an outstanding job of separating ourselves.

At the beginning of the week, my sense of betrayal was raw, my anger potent. I wanted nothing to do with him, so we reached an uncomfortable equilibrium. The games room and gazebo would be his work domain, while I took charge of the event room and other rooms upstairs.

Since that time, my anger has flared and dissipated while my sadness has only grown. To my surprise, I miss him. A lot. I miss his laugh and his banter and his warm presence. He puts everyone around him at ease, including me.

Sometimes, I forget that we're apart and I turn around to share a funny story with him, only to realize that he's nowhere to be found.

This isn't fun without him.

But then, why do I *care* if something is fun or not? Past Kiara from last year, or even last spring, would not have cared. Fun was for people who didn't have purpose.

The past week has felt like my old life, before the summer started. I've even stayed away from Bree, Anaya and Stefi. I've just been so focused on getting the right shot.

I step onto the balcony. The rain has let up, coming down as soft droplets instead of a torrential downpour. I stroll mindlessly to the edge of the railing and look towards the trees.

Now, I can see the gazebo through the trees. I spot Jonathan lining up a photo from outside the gazebo, looking in.

He's laughing, and a smile comes to my face. The question burning at the back of my mind will no longer be ignored.

Why do I miss him so much if it was all just a lie?

49

JONATHAN

"Okay wait, let me adjust this." One of the girls tugs the bottom of her dress. "How's that?"

She turns to her two friends and they nod and fiddle with their own dresses. I tune them out as they try to figure out the perfect pose for their social media platforms.

"Hey, what was your name again? Jacob?"

"Jonathan."

"Right." It's obvious she didn't register my name the second time around. "Can you stand over there, outside the gazebo, and we'll be on the stairs?"

I shrug and step out of the gazebo, standing under the trees. Thankfully, the rain has stopped for a moment.

"How's this?" one girl asks, making a goofy face.

I laugh and the other girls roll their eyes.

As I snap photos and follow their abrupt orders to move for better angles, it occurs to me that, last year, Troy and I would've been trying to pick up girls like them. They're smoking hot and they look to be only a year or two older than us.

But my heart isn't in it. All I can think about is Kiara.

Especially here, at the gazebo, where I caught her and her camera on our first day.

This week has been an absolute nightmare. And not only because the life-size cutout of Kade Monroe scares the pants off me every time I go in my cabin.

Sadness and self-doubt gnaw at me. I never got the impression that Kiara was holding me to a standard or that she had these high expectations of me. I never truly believed that she thought I was unfit to be a photographer.

But I was wrong.

I disappointed her in the end. When she mentioned that Isabella and I are perfect for each other, it became very clear that nothing has changed. She still sees me as the Edendale golden boy. Thought I was free from that label, but apparently not.

I have to return to Edendale in just over a week. I know that there's a ticking clock on Isabella keeping my secret. I need to tell everyone before she does. I can picture my parents' faces when they find out I came to the Inn instead of going to Momentum this summer.

And, even worse, that coming here was fruitless. The only thing I learned was that photography is not in my future. It's heartbreaking, and even more devastating to think of the mess I'll need to clean up in the aftermath.

"Thanks, Jacob!"

The girls flutter towards the Inn as the rain returns. I put my camera into its bag and stand in the gazebo, staring out over the lake.

What if I'm tired of trying to please everyone?

I suddenly feel angry, wondering why they're all dictating the path I follow in *my* life. Coming to the Inn was perhaps the only true decision that I, myself, made — in the memory of my grandpa who saw the best in me.

Ironically, the only person I can think of who makes decisions for herself is the very one who broke my heart.

Kiara made me stronger. She saw me for who I am, or who I thought I was. I miss her headstrong presence and her intelligence. Her stubborn, sometimes annoyingly so, confidence inspired me.

She told me to leave her alone, and that's what I've been doing. I've stayed far away from her at work and I've avoided her in the kitchen and staff room.

I've gotten closer with Anaya and Wes over the last few days, choosing to spend my time with them instead. But I see the expressions on their faces when they think I'm not looking. They worry about me and they ask me, in turns, if I'm okay.

As a seasoned "fake smiler", I think I'm getting away with it. But I feel a hole in my chest.

50

KIARA

*T*he bright sun shines through my window like an insult.

I put my pillow over my head, not ready to get up.

But the world is not accommodating to my moodiness. Birds chirp happily outside and some student workers are laughing. It's the first sun we've seen all week. At this moment, I actually prefer the rain.

I lay on my back, exasperated. My sleep has been fitful and restless for the past few days. I'm only functioning thanks to the fresh coffee Fernando makes every morning and afternoon.

Coffee. The thought revives me long enough to get out of bed and into fresh clothes.

I wander down the gravel path, squinting behind my sunglasses. A flash of color appears in the midst of the grey and I spot the little flower from my first day here, popping stubbornly through the gravel. It's bent over from the force of the rain and I lift it so it stands straight, adding a few rocks around it as a barrier.

"Morning Fernando!" I call out when I enter the staff room.

"Buongiorno, mi bella." He hands me a fresh cup of coffee.

"You're the only thing keeping me going these days."

I don't want to make Ava jealous, but Fernando and I are pretty much best friends.

I take a seat at the far end of the staff room, clicking open the photos on my camera. I scroll through my recent shots, wanting to see if I captured the moodiness of the weather over the last week. I practiced some black and white photos, and they turned out nice. Not all the photos are winners, but there are a few real, emotional gems.

I wonder if this is 'alive' enough for the Glacier Journal? I'm staring at an emotional photo of the peaks behind the lake appearing over a layer of fog. The white fog implies a lack of something, there's an air of mystery.

Thinking of the Glacier Journal fills me with unease. I haven't checked my emails since I last heard from my mom — I haven't felt brave enough. And now that Jonathan and I are no longer together, it seems pointless to check my email for the eventual rejection. I can only hope that they're not as harsh as they were with the last rejection.

I chug the rest of my coffee and walk into the event room, stationing myself by the windows.

As I gaze out over the lake, I think back to when I first entered this grand room. Back then, I followed Delia across the space and almost lost my breath trying to keep up. Since being at the Inn, I'm pleasantly surprised to see that my fitness level has increased. I still get horribly out of breath climbing to the Legacy summit, but it's not as bad as it used to be. All the explorations around the grounds have done more for my cardio than an entire year at the gym.

Well, I hope that's still the case. When was the last time I did a sunrise hike? A few weeks ago? It was before everything fell apart. I need to make it back to the Legacy summit before I go home next week.

"Good morning, dear!" Delia chortles, snapping me out of my thoughts. She's wearing her trademark black cowboy hat.

"Morning to you!"

"You're still cooped in the event room? It's not raining anymore. You should be outside! Why don't you head down to the gazebo and take some photos? Take advantage of the last of summer."

"I... I don't think it's a good idea for me to be down there."

Delia puts her hands on her hips. She's not used to being brushed off. "And why not?"

I fiddle with my camera and shift from foot to foot. I *really* don't want to get Delia involved in our drama, but I also don't want to work near Jonathan. I'm so embarrassed by what I said to him and how I treated him, but I also can't bear to hear about his relationship with Isabella. Telling Delia is probably the lesser of two evils.

"Jonathan and I aren't really working well together."

"So that's what you think, is it?"

What?

Delia takes off her cowboy hat and plucks a piece of lint from the brim. "Love and hate are two sides of the same coin, my dear. I'd suggest you two try flipping it again. Maybe it'll land on a different side."

Different side? My coffee hasn't hit, so I'm too tired to decipher what she means.

Delia stalks off without giving me an answer, exasperated.

"She's right, you know." Nath appears behind me, carrying a crazy-looking flowerpot towards the garden.

"About?" I'm still confused. It feels like everyone is talking around me this morning.

"Jonathan cares a lot about you. And you care a lot about him. You started out as rivals, became something more than friends, and now you're back to rivals. Who's to say another conversation won't change things? Who's to say you can't flip the coin again? Feelings don't just disappear."

My heart races and my mouth is dry. "But what about Isabella?"

"Pretty girl from the wedding? Smile like a shark that smells blood?"

"That's the one."

Nath bursts into laughter. "Your poor Jonathan made a deal with her. He gave her a dance in exchange for keeping a secret for him. Apparently, he's not supposed to be here."

"But she's his ex-girlfriend. And to use Delia's words, couldn't they just 'flip that coin' again?"

Nath places the flowerpot on the table. Her voice drops to her idle-gossip-about-movie-stars tone. "I don't think he's too interested in picking up that coin again. With you, on the other hand, it's a different story."

Nath gives me a friendly pat on the back, then picks up the flowerpot and disappears downstairs.

Meanwhile, I'm trying to process the whirlwind of emotions tossing me around. Could Nath be right — does he actually care about me? Did I pursue my passion for photography at the expense of someone I love?

As if on cue, Jonathan appears in the garden below. I watch as he helps Nath move a big table from one end of the garden to the other.

Did I make a mistake? My breath leaves me as he smiles at Nath and I'm hit by a profound sense of clarity.

Over the past summer, I've doubted my future, my photography, my dreams. But with Jonathan, everything felt clear. Everything felt alive. He's the perfect part of my day when everything feels softer and brighter. With him, darkness isn't so harsh.

He's my golden hour.

My heart races in my chest, and my eyes are wide open. He looks up towards the event room and I abruptly turn away.

It's the first time I've felt at peace since hearing about the competition for the headlining campaign. This competition now feels like an insignificant blip, a minor factor distracting from an even bigger truth.

I love Jonathan Wright. And I hope he can forgive me.

51

KIARA

I take the final step onto the Legacy summit, staring at my feet intently. Just as I used to do with Jonathan, I raise my head to take in the view in one panoramic glance. And just as I had done on many, many mornings this summer, I exhale in a whoosh. The sunrise this morning is breathtaking.

Laying down my rain jacket and taking a seat on the damp ground, I relish the view as the sun rises over the peaks behind the lake. Vibrant reds and yellows streak the sky, signaling a change of season. The horizon has a crispness to it, a brisk clarity. It felt like fall as I marched up the mountain. The cool breeze penetrated my light jacket, making me wish I brought a sweater.

For once, I'm up here alone.

I considered inviting Bree, or Stefi and Anaya, but it felt oddly intrusive to be up here with anyone other than Jonathan.

I tried to catch Jonathan. I wanted to invite him to the Legacy summit to chase sunrise for the last time. I couldn't, though, and if I'm honest, even if I got the chance to speak with him, I'm not sure what I would say.

The end is here. Tonight is our last night at Legacy Inn and we all head home tomorrow.

I take a sip of coffee from my to-go mug, the only accessory I have with me this morning. Climbing to the Legacy Summit by myself and without my camera was the perfect way to end a summer that had taught me so much.

"Wait til Ava hears about this." I gaze out over the horizon.

I'll admit that, despite my sadness, I'm beaming with pride at the fact that I did this alone. This was a feat that seemed impossible just three months ago.

But a lot of things seemed impossible three months ago.

Thinking back over the summer, I can't believe how much has changed. I came to the Legacy Inn afraid of bugs and taking "dull" photos. Now? Those fears have faded and my photos are alive.

I learned that photography can be fun. I learned that work doesn't always have to come ahead of play. And I learned that love can come first, even if — especially if — it feels scary.

All that being said, I wouldn't know where to begin explaining this to the person who most needs to hear it.

How do I put together the words to apologize to Jonathan? I abandoned him after Delia announced the competition, thinking only of myself when he had wanted to partner up. I accused him of not working hard for what he wants when I *know* that isn't the case. His being here this summer instead of at Momentum is a testament to that. Not to mention the fact that I assumed he and Isabella were back together without giving him the chance to explain.

The van Nispens would be so disappointed.

The sun is rising quickly over the peaks and the clouds are moving in, creating an even more dramatic skyline. As the peaks glow under the light, I think about the moments that changed my life the most this past summer.

I suddenly know what I need to do. Not only is it the right thing to do, but it's also the thing I want to do most.

52

JONATHAN

"Cheeseburger tacos or an avocado bagel?" Fernando booms as I approach him in the staff room.

He's wearing a tall chef's hat with massive blue sunglasses perched on the rim and a pink apron with flowers. He's really playing up the "last days of summer" theme.

"The usual, please!"

Fernando smirks and piles the bagel onto my plate. I walk over to a table with Stefi, Cooper, Anaya and Wes. Bree and Noah are nowhere to be found. It's a bittersweet moment as I remember how much Kiara loved these avocado bagels. It was her recipe that inspired Fernando to add the bagel to the menu.

"You look like my grandpa when he's on vacation," Anaya says.

"You can thank Vin for that," I say, laughing.

When he heard I was planning on wearing my regular hoodie and shorts, Vin lent me a bright yellow Hawaiian shirt. In true Legacy Inn fashion, our dinner theme is 'Last Days of Summer' so the outfit is basically mandatory. Our final guests left today and the staff leave tomorrow.

"Very... tropical." Anaya grins, then digs into her cheeseburger taco.

Her end of summer outfit is a massive beige sweater over a colorful sundress, with flip-flop earrings. It's quirky — perfect for her.

I hope we'll be friends once we all get back to school. It was fun to hang out with the kids from Edendale High without having labels attached.

Kiara enters the room and I nearly choke on my bagel.

She wears a white blouse and red capri pants. Her hair falls in soft waves, and she's practically glowing. She walks to Fernando — completely unaware of the effect she's having on me — and laughs with him. She almost does the little half-smile that I love so much, and I briefly wonder if I'll be lucky enough to see it again.

She turns, her eyes meeting mine. There's something there, an invisible spark, and then she looks away.

I'm no longer hungry. All I want is to see her smile.

Anything to make her happy.

And I know of one thing that *will* make her happy — winning the competition to work as the Inn's official photographer.

The last few days have been eye-opening. I've realized that I don't need to live by other people's expectations. Photography is my dream, but I know I need the extra education. Photography school is my future, and winning the competition would guarantee entry, but I won't do it if it means hurting Kiara. She's spent her life building her portfolio, I've only worked through the summer.

Tonight, after our dinner, I plan to tell Delia that Kiara will headline the campaign. It's the least I can do for her, regardless of if she ever wants to speak to me again.

"Hi, everyone, hello." Kiara stands on a chair at the front of the room.

The room goes silent and everyone turns towards her.

What is she doing?

"Thanks." There's a nervous wobble in her voice. "I've just got a few things to say, then we can all go back to stuffing our faces."

Anaya, mid-bite, chuckles and almost chokes. She pats herself on the chest, then motions for Kiara to continue. This gives Kiara courage, and her trademark half-smile returns.

My heart wants to burst.

"This has been the best summer of my life," Kiara says. "I want to say a special thanks to Vin and Nath for showing me the ropes, and to Delia for her never-ending guidance and happy spirit. I'll never forget the time we all spent together."

A chorus of "aww"s are heard throughout the room.

"There is one person, in particular, that I want to thank," Kiara says. She takes a deep breath. "Jonathan Wright. When I saw you here on our first day, I was... devastated."

Everyone laughs, and I snort despite my confusion. Yes, I remember that clearly.

"But you showed me so much this summer. I learned a lot thanks to you. Not only in terms of photography but also in terms of life. You have to be one of the most fun, most irresponsible, most carefree people I know. And I love that about you."

Did she just—

"And because of that — because you've already taught me so much — I want to return the favor."

Kiara turns towards Delia, who's standing at the back of the room.

It's difficult to breathe.

"Delia, Jonathan should headline the Inn's ad campaign in the coming months. He's done some *phenomenal* work and I couldn't be happier to see what he's achieved. I want to give up my spot in the competition."

53

KIARA

*T*he entire room stares at me, but I feel confident. Normally, I don't do well speaking in front of crowds. But I've thought about this moment so many times that the words come easily.

When I realized I needed to give up my spot, a weight lifted. Jonathan deserves this opportunity, and I'm tired of competing with him for it. I've done what I can with my portfolio and, in all honesty, I'm proud of what I've accomplished this summer.

Because of Jonathan, my photos are alive. There's movement, there's excitement, there's a genuine sense of liveliness. Whether or not Glacier Journal agrees, I know my photos are miles ahead of where they once were.

Now, it's his turn to build a portfolio he's proud of, so he can pursue what he truly wants to do.

My eyes meet Delia's. Instead of nodding or acknowledging my speech, she's simply beaming at me, for some bizarre reason.

Before either of us can say anything, Jonathan stands and leaves the room.

Silence echoes throughout the space and devastation fills me. My hands fall to my side and the room hesitantly breaks out into a low chatter.

Nice one, Kiara.

Sadness consumes me. I guess I'm too late, after all.

Nath stands and makes her way towards me, along with Anaya and Stefi. Delia's disappeared.

I give my friends a half-wave, then bolt down the stairs, away from the Inn.

The tears come hot and heavy as I dart to my cabin, hoping that Jonathan didn't come this way. Or maybe hoping he did. It's clear that our relationship is over. Officially, this time.

I slip into my cabin and slam the door, then collapse on the floor and let the tears flow. In Jonathan's eyes, I'm back to being 'Kiara the Queen' and he's back to being 'Golden Boy.' Come next Monday, we'll be at Edendale High, lobbing insults from afar.

I made a mistake.

I followed my fear instead of listening to my heart. All of my most treasured moments this summer included Jonathan. These moments were special because of *him*, not because of the wildlife and nature, or the weddings, or even the photography.

Mom was wrong. It was never about finding time for love, but about making time for love when it found you.

I wipe away my tears, grab my suitcase, and start stuffing clothes inside. I've done everything I need to do at Legacy Inn. There's no point in me staying for the last day. Jonathan's made it abundantly clear how he feels about me. I don't particularly want to stick around and face him. I'll be doing enough of that over this final year at Edendale High.

There should be buses running early tomorrow. I press

my little black dress into my suitcase and resolve to hop on the first bus. Knowing my mom, she won't be around, so I'll have a few days to mope before school starts.

I put my suitcase on the floor and turn off the light in my cabin for the last time. I glance around the room as a stupid part of me wishes that Jonathan might change his mind, might come and find me.

I tuck myself into my bed, bringing my blanket right under my chin as the tears slide sideways down my face. Up until I fall asleep, I wish to hear a knock on my door. We don't need to get back together; I just want him to forgive me.

But the knock never comes, and each moment throws me deeper into an unpleasant sleep.

54

JONATHAN

*I*t's almost time. I hope this works.

My heart races as I walk through the darkness around the cabins. A layer of dew covers the grass, but I barely notice my soaking shoes. I gingerly make my way into my cabin, grab a single item, then exit.

A small strip of grass separates my cabin from Kiara's. I stand near the window and summon my courage.

Knock. Knock.

My knuckles rap lightly against the glass and I listen for any sign of life in the cabin. But there's only silence.

I knock again, slightly louder. This time, I hear a soft moan and some movement from inside the cabin. Overhead, the dark sky is taking on a bluish hue.

I knock one last time.

The curtains slide open.

Kiara glares, her hair piled high onto her head. Somehow, she's still one of the most beautiful people I've ever seen. I motion for her to open the window, and reluctantly, she does.

"Come with me," I whisper. I repeat the words that tied

us together before our first cliff jump. "Trust me. One more time. Please."

She narrows her eyes.

My heart beats so loudly the noise will surely wake the entire Inn. She has no reason to trust me, but I'm hoping luck might swing in my favor.

She closes the window and shuts the curtains.

I take a step back. A decision has been made, but which way will it go?

I wait.

And wait.

And wait.

My hopes crash and burn. She won't be coming with me. She put herself out there, took a leap of faith, and I wasn't there to catch her. Now she's—

Her cabin door opens. She steps out wearing a hoodie and shorts.

I smile, bound over to her, and grab her hand. She doesn't intertwine her fingers with mine, but she doesn't pull away, either.

It takes two steps for her to figure out where we're going.

This morning, we reach the Legacy summit in record time. Without saying a word, we look at each other, silently count to three, then lift our heads to take in the scene in one look. Together.

55

JONATHAN

The Legacy summit is a mirror image of our first date. There's a blanket for us to sit, and the spot is lit by candles. The sky is still dark blue, so the effect is especially pronounced. The air is calm, and it feels like we're up in space, above the entire world.

Kiara takes in the scene and her adorable half-smile returns. She lets go of my hand, wordlessly moves to the blanket, and pats the spot next to her.

I sit.

She shivers.

I hand her the coffee mug I brought up.

Still not saying anything, but now grinning, she wraps her hands around it. She takes a sip, her eyes gazing into mine, waiting for me to talk. She told me her truth in the staff room, and now it's time for me to return the favor.

How on earth am I going to get the words right?

"This summer has been everything," I say. "I've never met someone so stubborn."

She cocks an eyebrow, but she's still grinning.

"Someone so stubborn, and so brilliant. And confident. And headstrong."

She sets her coffee down and takes my hands. She rubs one of her thumbs along mine.

"I don't care about being the Inn's official photographer. I don't care about the Eagles. Or Edendale. I don't care about any of that, because none of that means anything if I can't be with you. This whole insane competition doesn't matter to me if it means losing you. I'm going to tell Delia I'm stepping down."

Her mouth twitches, but she still says nothing.

"At the wedding, Isabella asked me to dance in exchange for not telling anyone that I was here." It's hard to look Kiara in the eye, but I do my best. "And that's one of my biggest regrets. I love photography, and I shouldn't be trying to keep it a secret. You should never keep the things you love a secret. And that's why I don't want to keep you a secret. To keep us a secret. If there's still an us — and I'm really hoping there is."

Every word is true.

The sun rises slowly, the sky a swirl of beautiful pastels. A late summer breeze surrounds us with the scent of pine. The candles flicker.

"I came up here alone yesterday," Kiara says, her voice barely above a whisper. "Because of you, I'm climbing mountains in the dark. And not just because it makes a great photo op. But because I want to. Because life is about climbing mountains and taking chances and living."

I squeeze her hands.

"I'm so sorry for what I said," Kiara says. "I know how hard you work. I know how difficult it must have been for you to come here. You stood up to the world to pursue something you love."

My heart sings. Kiara always speaks the truth. She continues. "You have done something amazing this summer, Jonathan. And you never cease to amaze me."

"But," I say. "I still have one regret."

She raises her eyebrows.

"I didn't get to dance with you at the wedding."

She stands, her half-smile on her face. "So dance with me now."

I stand and take her in my arms. She wraps her arms around my neck and rests her head on my chest. We sway side to side to a soundless rhythm that only we can hear. I feel the warmth of her body and smell the shampoo in her hair. She fits perfectly in my arms.

"I love you, Kiara."

She tilts her head. "And I you."

Slowly, I take her face in my hand. I want to extend this perfect moment for as long as possible. As we slow dance on the mountaintop, the sun rising, the sky a vibrant collection of colors, my lips meet hers. We kiss with the softness of whispered secrets, and there's a profound sense of peace.

She pulls away, a smile on her face. She takes my camera from its bag and holds it out in front of us.

"Say Legacy!"

She smiles, and right before the shutter clicks, I kiss her on the cheek. She scrunches her face and laughs.

No matter where life takes us, I know that the world is better when Kiara is by my side.

56

KIARA

"*J*ump!" I squeal and take a deep breath.

I run towards the ledge and then, at the last moment, hold back. Jonathan flies through the air ahead of me, plunging into the freezing water below. He surfaces and I'm almost falling over laughing.

He laughs when he sees that I've tricked him. "Think you're so funny? I'm going to get you."

We've been playing around in the canyon for a long while, trying to take advantage of our final few hours at the Inn. It's a warm August day, thankfully, but the water is chilly.

I stick my tongue out at him and do a little dance on the perch, my eyes glancing on cardboard Kade, staring at us intensely from behind a bush.

Never one to admit defeat, Jonathan squeezed in one last prank. This morning, after watching the sunrise on Legacy summit, he took my hand and led me back to the canyon, just as we used to do earlier in the summer. My entire being felt warm, happy, at peace.

Until I saw it.

He led me onto the perch and I was getting ready to lean in for a kiss when I noticed a pair of dark eyes staring at us.

I jerked away from him as I processed the shocking scene.

"What the?!"

Kade Monroe was staring at us from behind a bush. Holding a snake.

I instinctively took a step back, my breath catching. But, of course, I stepped into thin air.

When I surfaced in the water, bobbing and spluttering, Jonathan was keeled over laughing. He had his arm around Kade. That's when I realized that golden boy had somehow fashioned a life-sized cardboard version of Kade Monroe.

Now, I screech as he hops out of the water and runs full tilt up the side of the canyon, grabbing my arm and wrapping me in a massive bear hug. Within moments, I'm pressed up against his very cold and wet body.

"See, it's not so bad."

His voice is low as he looks into my eyes. I suddenly don't want to laugh anymore. He runs his fingers through my hair and kisses me, leaving me breathless.

He takes me in his arms and I've never felt so happy. This just feels right.

Or so I thought.

He gazes into my eyes, and I see a glimmer of... something.

Something suspicious.

I suddenly realize his plan and try to wriggle out of his grasp. It's too late.

With me in his arms, he runs towards the edge of the perch. I let out a scream as we both fly through the air, landing in the water with a massive splash.

When I rise to the surface, I can't stop laughing. I grab his hand and pull him to me, trying to steal his warmth.

His hands run along my arms and down my sides, leaving a trail of goosebumps. I circle my arms around his neck and kiss him deeply.

Eventually, we head back to our cabins to get ready for lunch. Delia will make her final announcements before we all head home. I quickly grab my shorts and a hoodie from my packed bag, unable to keep the smile off my face.

"So..." Jonathan asks as we stroll hand in hand down the gravel path towards the Inn. "How does it feel to have obliterated me in the social media post competition this summer?"

"I'm surprised I didn't kick your butt a little more." I grin. "But it feels pretty good, golden boy."

Jonathan and I ended up being very close in terms of photos posted on the Inn's social media accounts. I beat him by a margin of 10 posts, which isn't a lot in the grand scheme.

"I guess you *are* pretty good though," I say, rolling my eyes teasingly.

He raises our clasped hands to kiss the back of mine. "All thanks to you."

I'm laughing when Jonathan stops abruptly. He bends down and replaces a rock that had fallen from around the barrier surrounding the little pink flower. It's still surviving through the gravel, thriving.

We stroll into the staff room, our hands clasped, and all the staffers smile our way. None of them look particularly surprised. I think about the debacle from last night and blush. But it's okay — this group really has become a bit of a family over the last few months.

Jonathan and I grab lunch and take a seat at a table. To

my surprise, the room is almost empty. I'm wondering what happened to all of the student workers when I notice that Jonathan is distracted, staring around the room.

"What's up?" I ask as I dig into an avocado bagel.

"Nothing." Jonathan says, but he continues looking around the room. "I'm trying to find Delia."

"Why?"

He sits back in his chair, exasperated. Delia is nowhere to be found, but her announcements will start soon. "I'm going to tell her you'll be headlining the ad campaign, not me."

I freeze, my bagel halfway to my mouth. I'm about to protest when he continues.

"Seriously, Kiara, you've earned this. You've worked so hard your entire life for this kind of opportunity. I can't be the one standing in your way."

"Jonathan." I put down my bagel, my voice stern. "You will not do that. You've *earned* this and you've worked hard for it. You have a real talent for photography, I knew it when I saw you taking that photo at the Eagles game. Everything I showed you this summer was just... extra. You deserve this."

I smile as I continue. "But what you showed me this summer? Helping me live in the moment and all that? It's priceless to me. It's the best thing I could've ever expected from this summer. You *should* win this headlining campaign."

Jonathan's eyes show his uncertainty, but I've never been surer in my life. I give him a kiss on the cheek and squeeze his hand.

"Trust me," I whisper.

Delia enters and stands on a chair at the front of the room.

JONATHAN

"*G*ood afternoon!" Delia calls out and the room immediately goes quiet.

I break my eyes away from Kiara's. She wants me to trust her, so I will. I hold her hand tightly and listen to Delia.

"Today is our last day at the Legacy Inn after another successful summer. We did it!"

The room breaks into applause and cheers.

"I want to thank each and every one of you for the vital role you've played this summer. We have so many positive reviews to share, along with some special shoutouts. Vin's compiled a slideshow of some key Legacy Inn moments — using the work of our star photographers, of course." Delia gestures towards us.

Another round of applause erupts across the room.

I'm beaming, incredibly proud. I mock-bow towards Kiara, and she's blushing fiercely, laughing along.

"And on that, it's time to share who we've selected to be the winner of our big headlining competition. The winning photographer will be redoing all the Inn's imagery for our international ad campaign. It's an incredible opportunity to showcase your work around the world — and contribute something to your savings account." Delia winks theatrically and everyone chuckles.

I squeeze Kiara's hand. I'm feeling uneasy — I don't want to take this opportunity from her.

She looks at me, her eyes calm. She's made her decision and doesn't have any regrets. She runs her thumb along mine.

"Vin and I had a tremendously hard time trying to decide. Kiara tried to forfeit her spot last night, but unfortunately, we'd already made our decision."

I smile and squeeze her hand. She's the winner. It had to be her, and I'm so excited for what this means for her future.

She stares at Delia, her mouth open.

"And, in keeping with the magic of Legacy Inn, we wanted to make this fun!" Delia clicks aggressively on the remote, trying to get the slideshow to appear on the screen at the front of the room. "The first few photos on the slideshow demonstrate some of the winner's amazing work — ugh, Vin, this darned remote isn't working."

"Have you tried clicking it harder?" Vin jogs to the front of the room while the staff chuckle. After a couple minutes of fidgeting, he returns to his position next to Nath.

"Fantastic." Delia gets back on track. "Without further ado, here is the work of our winner!"

The first photo appears on the screen and I immediately recognize the shot.

The photo was taken on our first day here, capturing the arrival of the first guests. It almost looks like a stock image — the happy family is walking up the gravel path, their faces lit with excitement.

I remember that moment. Kiara had just teased me about being late. The photo is clearly hers.

Looking at her now, she's shocked, staring at the screen with her mouth popped open. We've come so far, the two of us. I can't describe how proud I feel for her, and for her future. It's exactly what she's worked so hard for.

"Congratulations," I whisper excitedly, kissing her on the cheek.

She snaps out of her shock and smiles at me, but instead of looking excited, her eyes are sad.

"What's wrong?" I whisper as the next photo appears on the screen.

The room bursts into applause at the image. This one is of the sunrise. Our first morning on the Legacy summit. It's a captivating shot, made all the sweeter by the memory that we had our first meaningful conversation on the mountain that very morning.

"I wanted it to be you," Kiara whispers.

I wrap my arm around her and kiss the top of her head as the applause fades. "Next time."

The next photo on the screen is one I know very, very well.

I frown as recognition hits me. The photo is of the twin girls laughing in front of the dock. It was the photo I took after placing the fake spider on Kiara's head.

Wait. But...

What?

The next photo appears.

This one is of Kiara gazing towards the sunset, her expression perfectly betraying her thoughts.

Another one of mine?

Kiara's confused, too.

Obviously, there's been a mistake.

We both turn towards Delia and she's beaming at us like she's just told the world's funniest joke.

I clear my throat to try and explain. "Delia, those photos—"

"We've decided to hire *both* of you!"

WHAT?

She clicks her remote.

A page with two photos appears — a candid shot of Kiara laughing, and the sunrise from the Legacy summit. One of mine, one of hers.

"The universe saw fit to bless us with two talented photographers this summer. Jonathan, this shot of Kiara pulled my heart strings and perfectly captured the romanticism and magic of the Inn. And Kiara, your photo of the sunrise shows the life of the world around the Inn."

My heart stops. Kiara's hand is limp in mine.

"Both of these photos will be featured as part of the ad campaign. And you both will be working with us to headline the campaign internationally. If you're okay working as a team, that is."

Kiara laughs and gazes into my eyes. "I'd be delighted. He still has a thing or two to learn, after all."

"Likewise," I say. "Someone's got to be there to catch her camera when she drops it."

Kiara playfully swats me on the shoulder, then leans in and gives me a quick kiss.

We're showered with applause and congratulations.

My heart thumps and a happy excitement overwhelms me. This year, Kiara and I will not only study together at Edendale High, we'll also work together for Legacy Inn.

Imagine. Doing what we love the most in the place where we fell for each other.

58

JONATHAN

"Come on, golden boy. How are you so disorganized?"

Kiara sits on my bed wearing one of my favorite hoodies. It looks great on her, and I wonder whether I'll ever get it back. Probably not.

"We didn't all get a ridiculously early head start and pack last night," I say.

"Hmm, this is true." She flops back onto the bed dramatically. "I almost hopped on a bus and got out of here first thing this morning. It's lucky for you that I waited."

She says this with a note of humor in her voice, but my heart hurts a little at the thought. I give her a kiss before I return to packing my suitcase.

"Sure is."

We talk about everything and nothing as I finish packing. But we mostly talk about what the next few months will look like working for the Inn on top of our senior classes. Kiara has some wonderful ideas and I can't wait to help her capture the images she's dreaming of.

"It'll be interesting too, once we're back in Edendale," she says carefully as our talk turns to school. "Are you sure you won't mind being seen with the Edendale High outcast? The 'Queen' of school?" She says this theatrically, making quotation marks with her fingers.

"I've never been surer of anything."

Kiara gives me her half-smile and I feel excited for what the next few months, and years, will bring us.

I turn back to my dresser and check every drawer. It's only then that I realize I forgot some precious cargo in the bottom drawer. I hesitantly take out my shin guards and cleats, the gear that I'd stashed away months ago.

"It's been ages since I thought about soccer." I look at my jerseys. "I kind of miss it."

Kiara comes over to me, giving me a hug. "Makes sense, you have been playing it for years."

I pack my soccer gear on top, feeling oddly sad. I don't miss all the stuff surrounding soccer. I don't miss my stressed family, my nagging coach, my intense teammates. But I miss the sport, I miss the game. Soccer is a part of me and I don't know that it will ever go away, even if I choose another path for my future.

Suddenly, Kiara gives a little squeak and bounds out of the cabin. I zip up my suitcase and place it by the door, hurrying after her.

When I get onto my balcony, she's disappeared. I stare around the property, trying to see her, but all I can see are staffers tying up loose ends and packing everything away. The student cabins next to us are surprisingly quiet and I wonder where the other Edendale High kids have gone.

Kiara pops out from underneath her cabin. She shakes herself off and then drops a very familiar object onto the green grass.

"Ready for me to kick your butt again, Jonathan

Wright?" She kicks the ball around the green space near our cabins.

I grin, hop down from my balcony, and race towards her. I steal the ball, dart around her, and make her chase me a bit, laughing.

That's when she full-on body-checks me and steals the ball back.

"Red card! Red card!"

"No ref to save you here, golden boy!" She darts towards a pretend goal.

I chase after her, but before I can stop her, she makes a final kick and sends the ball flying through the air towards the hammocks.

"Goooooooaaaaaaaaal!" She falls to her knees, her arms up in the sky.

I fall beside her, laughing, take her in my arms, and kiss her.

59

JONATHAN

"*J*onathan Wright!"

A very familiar, very deep voice stops me cold. I get off the ground and help Kiara up. Holding her hand, I turn to face my parents.

"Mom. Dad." My voice is a croak. "What are you doing here?"

My dad's mouth twitches and the blood vessel along his temple looks like it'll burst.

Mom doesn't look much happier. "We should ask you the same thing."

"What have you been doing?" Dad shouts. "How long have you been here?"

Mom steps in front of dad, her arms crossed, her voice shrill. "We suspected something was wrong when we didn't hear from you for a few days and we reached out to Troy. After a few phone calls, he finally admitted that you were here and *not* at Momentum. He said you spent the summer here? Tell me it's not true."

I stare at the ground, feeling lost. The resolution and certainty I felt just a few minutes ago has dissipated. The disappointment in my parents' voices stings like a cut from the sharpest knife.

Then, Kiara squeezes my hand and I know that she's here with me. It gives me strength.

"It's true," I say, my voice firmer than I feel. "I lied to you about going to Momentum. I know that I should be sorry... but I'm not."

"You're. Not. Sorry?" Dad's nostrils flare.

"I didn't want things to go this way." I keep my voice level. "But I knew I had to do this, and I didn't think you'd understand. Remember when Grandpa Wright gave me that camera a year ago? The same camera that you made me hide in my closet last fall?"

My parents nod curtly, their rage still evident.

I continue. "He gave me the camera because I told him I liked photography. He was the only one who listened."

My mom's face softens almost imperceptibly. We all loved Grandpa Wright, our entire family was devastated when he passed away this spring. I take a deep breath as I push on, finally getting the truth off my chest.

"My love for soccer died a long time ago. I don't want to pursue it anymore. I don't want the stupid scholarship. I want to play soccer because I enjoy it and it's fun, not because it's my 'life's purpose'."

I squeeze Kiara's hand and my mom registers the movement. Her face softens even more.

"So I skipped out on Momentum. I came to the Legacy Inn at the last minute to work as a photographer. That's where I want my future to be." I take a deep breath, ready to deal the final blow. "When I graduate, I'll be going to photography school."

My voice is firm, and the world feels silent as my parents

process my decision. I look over at Kiara and her eyes are encouraging. No matter what, I'll be okay.

"We've only ever wanted the best for you," Dad says. His voice isn't hard, isn't on edge. "We thought soccer was the best thing. It would get you into a great school, a full-ride. A better school than we could afford."

My mom takes my dad's hand, her voice gentle. "We're sorry that we placed so much on you. We thought you wanted it as much as we did. But if you don't, that's okay."

A heavy weight lifts from my chest, and I can breathe again.

"But lying to us all summer?" Dad's voice is firm, betrayed.

"That," I say, "I am sorry for. I just didn't know what else to do."

My parents are silent.

Will they forgive me? Our relationship has become really complicated over the last few years, but I want to believe that the happy parents from my childhood are still there.

"Next time, can you at least talk to us before you go gallivanting off to the middle of nowhere?" Mom's voice carries a smile, and when I look up, my parents look... happy. Like how they used to be.

My face breaks into a wide, hesitant smile. "I promise."

60

KIARA

"*I*'m home!" I call out automatically to the empty house. I place my keys in the bowl by the front door and drop my bag.

Jonathan and his parents gave me a ride back to town so I didn't have to take the bus. His parents are intense, but lovely. They were overjoyed to hear that we both got positions as photographers for the Inn. That should help take the stress off the finances for Jonathan's college education. He held my hand the entire way home, and I couldn't stop smiling.

Sebastian rounds the corner. There's a bit of pudge to him, like someone strapped an extra stick of butter to his belly.

"Hello, sir. Looks like mom kept you well-fed, hey?"

"You better believe it!" A voice calls from the kitchen.

Mom?

She's actually home for once?

I hurry to the kitchen.

Mom is wearing an apron and standing over the stove.

She comes over to me and gives me a big hug. "I'm so glad to see you!"

I hug her back. "What are you doing here?"

She laughs, releases me, and heads back to the stove, her hair loose down her back. She's wearing casual pants and a bright t-shirt — a major change from her creased work pants and blouses. "I wanted to make our favorite dinner for your first night back."

I stare at her, skeptical.

She turns off the stove and drains the water from the pot into the sink. "Oh, fine. Echo completed a project today, so I took the evening off. But I did want to see you."

Her voice is sincere. She ladles mac and cheese onto two plates, along with a side salad dripping with balsamic vinaigrette.

"It's nice to see you," I say, heading to the dining table. And it is — it's a pleasant surprise.

She brings our plates over, humming softly.

I smile — I owe my incessant mumbling and humming to her.

She sits. "Tell me everything!"

We dig into the mac and cheese and I start telling her about my summer at Legacy Inn. I'm in the middle of describing Delia — and there's so much to describe — when I catch sight of a thick manila envelope on the counter. The logo?

Glacier Journal.

I leap from the table. "What's this?"

"It came in the mail yesterday," Mom says.

My heart races. The envelope, it's thicker than the one they use for a rejection letter. Could it be?

I rip it open and skim the piece of paper inside.

My heart drops.

Dear Kiara,

Thank you for your recent submission. We'd love to publish your photo in the next issue of Glacier Journal! Our magazine is built around this style of photography and if you have any similar shots, we'd enjoy collaborating with you.

"No way."

"What?" Mom rushes over and peeks at the paper over my shoulder. "Did you—"

"I'M GETTING PUBLISHED!" My voice is so loud I'm sure Delia can hear it all the way back at Legacy Inn.

Mom wraps her arms around me, and I almost collapse.

My heart beats so fast I think I might faint.

I did it.

I actually did it.

I pull out a second piece of paper from the envelope. It's a printed copy of the photo I submitted — the sunrise from Legacy summit. I remember every detail of that morning. It was the first time I realized I loved Jonathan.

Mom's jaw drops. "That's breathtaking. How did you..."

Grinning, I return to my place at the table. "Mom, let me tell you all about Legacy Inn, and the boy who changed everything."

61

KIARA

"*H*ey Ki!" A voice calls out as I walk down the hallway. It's my first day of senior year, a year I'm sure I'll never forget.

Ava runs towards me, lugging her violin case.

I give her a big hug. "I missed you!"

"Really?" She raises an eyebrow. "I didn't miss you at all — wait."

Ava steps back and sizes me up. "WAIT. Ki, are you wearing... mascara?"

I burst out laughing and take one of her bags. "The mountains have changed me."

Ava links her arm in mine, and we walk down the hallway. Ava fills me in on her summer at band camp. When she's finished, she turns to me expectantly. "Now your turn."

I take a deep breath and launch into a shortened version of my summer at Legacy Inn. Ava's eyes grow wider and wider as I speak, her mouth dropping open.

"Jonathan Wright? Into photography?" She shakes her head in disbelief. "Those mountains must be made of magic."

I open my phone and show her the photo he took of me laughing. He took it the day I helped the elderly lady move her chair on the dock. It's the same photo the Inn wants to use for the ad campaign.

"Okay, wow, that's actually pretty good," Ava says. "Not as good as you, of course."

I laugh. "It's okay. We're a team."

She gives my arm a light slap. "Pretty sure you're more than a team."

"Maybe."

There's a familiar burst of laughter from down the hall. Jonathan and Troy turn the corner and Jonathan's eyes light up when he sees me. He nudges Troy and they walk over to us.

I called Jonathan right after dinner when I got the news from Glacier Journal. He came over immediately to congratulate me and, in doing so, met my mom. He stayed for a little while and we recounted the events from the summer.

After he left, Mom wrapped me in a hug, and told me she approved.

Now, my legs are turning to jelly as he gets closer, my heart beating fast. He takes me in his arms and kisses me in front of everyone. I'm happy to see that he's wearing a hoodie today instead of his usual polo shirt. I wonder how long it'll be before I can steal it.

"How's the Queen?"

I put on my best formal voice. "She is most pleased by your attendance."

We both burst out laughing, and our laughter is interrupted by none other than Isabella, strutting down the hallway. Lucas follows her like he's being pulled on a leash.

"Wow," Isabella says. "Edendale's golden boy is making a move for the throne. How depressingly predictable. But I suppose you were out in the mountains, and no one else was around, so..."

Jonathan shrugs. "Is that why you were making moves on that college boy at your cousin's wedding? Because no one else was around?"

Isabella's jaw drops.

Lucas freezes.

Jonathan's voice carries through the hallway, and everyone has stopped to stare.

Lucas looks to Jonathan, to Isabella, then to Jonathan again. "What?"

Isabella puts her hand on her hip and flips her hair. "Well, if we're trading secrets—"

Jonathan laughs. "And what secret do you think you have on me? That I skipped Momentum? That I'm a photographer for Legacy Inn? It's not much of a secret — I'm listed on their website, and I've already handed in my kit to Coach."

I wrap my arm around his waist. "Your move, Izzy."

Isabella lets out a frustrated bleat and stomps away, Lucas following close behind her. The argument escalates. Someone says something nasty, then a new argument starts — it sounds like they're arguing over who's breaking up with whom.

Jonathan grabs my hand and the four of us walk to our first class.

We pass Bree as she puts her books away in her locker. She turns around and gives us a wave, smiling brightly. I wave back, hoping to catch up with her later. She missed the last day at the Inn and I wondered whether she was okay. She looks happy now... I wonder what happened with her and Noah this summer, anyway?

I rub my thumb along Jonathan's as I tune back into the

conversation. He's telling Troy and Ava about the ad campaign we got with the Inn. I pipe in to say that we start working next week and the two of them give us big hugs.

"You're going to have to step up your game this year, bro. I won't be around to bail you out." Jonathan jokes, punching Troy lightly on the arm.

"Were you even on the team last year?" Troy asks. "I don't remember you *playing* in any of the games."

Jonathan and Troy banter.

Ava links her arm in mine. "I don't want to alarm you, Ki, but you're smiling like an idiot."

"You're probably right," I say, "only an idiot would fall in love with Jonathan Wright."

We laugh and I begin to think about the years ahead. Jonathan and I have made a plan. Together. He'll apply for photography schools in the countries I most want to visit. Wherever he gets in is where we'll live.

With Jonathan by my side, the world is open and exciting. I can't wait for the future, wherever it takes us.

PLEASE LEAVE A REVIEW

If you enjoyed reading this book, I'd appreciate it if you were able to leave a review.

Reviews help authors get noticed and they can bring my books to the attention of other readers who may enjoy them.

Thank you so much!

—Sara Jane

ALSO BY SARA JANE WOODLEY

The Summer I Fell for My Best Friend

The Summer I Fell for My Fake Boyfriend

www.ingramcontent.com/pod-product-compliance
Lightning Source LLC
Chambersburg PA
CBHW022111240626
47153CB00007B/2320